SPIRIT OF THE WOLF

Sloppy's Secrets

Volume 3

RANDY HOGUE

Copyright © 2024 by Randy Hogue

All rights reserved. No part of this publication may be reproduced, stored in a retrieval system or transmitted, in any form, or by any means, electronic, mechanical, recorded, photocopied, or otherwise, without the prior written permission of both the copyright owner and the publisher, except by a reviewer who may quote brief passages in a review.

The scanning, uploading, and distribution of this book via the Internet or via any other means without the permission of the publisher is illegal and punishable by law. Please purchase only authorized electronic editions and do not participate in or encourage piracy of copywritten material.

This is a work of fiction. Names, characters, places and incidents either are a product of the author's imagination or are used fictitiously, and any resemblance to actual persons, living or dead, business establishments, events, or locales is purely coincidental.

This book may contain views, premises, depictions, and statements by the author that are not necessarily shared or endorsed by Outlaws Publishing.

For information contact: info@outlawspublishing.com
Cover Art by Randy Hogue
Cover design by Outlaws Publishing.
Published by Outlaws Publishing.
September 2024
10 9 8 7 6 5 4 3 2 1

"We make a living

By what we get

But we make a life

By what we give"

Winston Churchill

Dedication:

To my lifelong friend Hank 'Sloppy' Floyd. Sloppy passed away in 2014, but the character in this story reminds me of him.

Acknowledgement:

Thanks to Tom Pilgrim for directing me to Outlaws Publishing.

And thanks to Jan Roberts for her continued help with these stories.

To my granddaughter Evie McGovern for doing the computer work, Paw Paw thanks you.

Foreword:

Sloppy's Secrets takes you into the life and secrecy of a man whose true desire was to live his life high up in the rugged terrain of the Appalachian Mountains in a little cabin. His love of the mountains brought him happiness, difficulties and sorrow at times over the next forty-five years.

A long-lasting friendship was forged with the Adams' family and their lives became intertwined. A strong bond of trust and love developed and with no family of his own, he became a beloved member of their family. Sloppy's bond with young Yano Adams plays a pivotal role in his future.

The author, in this compelling story, shines a spotlight on the mysterious life of a true mountain man, the lessons he taught, the treasures he collected, the many secrets he kept and the heart wrenching gift he gave so freely to a young girl.

Sloppy had many untold secrets until…

CHAPTER I

On a warm sunny day in the Appalachian Mountains, Sloppy was planning on leaving the Adams' homestead and going back to his place in the mountains for a couple of weeks. He stays with the Adams every time he comes out of the mountains for supplies he needs in town and to sell his pelts or any gold he had prospected. After seventeen years of friendship, the Adams consider him kin folks and love it when he stays with them for months at a time.

It's July 3, 1865, and it's the twins, Ayita and Koda's birthday. Sloppy wanted to stay and celebrate their birthday before leaving. Ayita and Koda were twelve years old and Sloppy had secretly prepared a gift for each of them. He made each one of them a small wooden box with their names carved on top of the lid. Inside each box, he put a cloth tobacco bag inside with gemstones. Along with the gemstones of turquoise, emeralds and rubies, he also put five gold nuggets of equal size in each bag. Ayita and Koda were very grateful for their gifts from Sloppy. At twelve years old, they may not know the true value of such a gift, but to them, it was priceless. It pleased Sloppy's heart to see the smile on their faces.

Tehya Bolin had baked two birthday cakes for Ayita and Koda and her daughter Nova delivered them for them to enjoy. Alan and Odina were all smiles watching the twins celebrate their twelfth birthday, always remembering how Ayita almost didn't make it past her seventh. Yano and Nokomis were also enjoying a piece of the cake Tehya had baked for the twins.

At approximately seventy-three years old, Sloppy could not stay at his place in the mountains for too long at a time now because of his health, but he still loved it and he had more secret things he needed to get in order. More secrets to be found after he was gone.

The Adams loved having Sloppy stay with them in the shanty they called his place and wished he would stay all the time, so they could look after him. They worried about him when he went back to the mountains because it was so far with no one around for miles if he should need help, but they completely understood his love for that kind of life.

Alan was still working at the Stockburn Coal Mining Company in Rockford and had stayed three years longer than he had promised he would. He still loved the coal mining business, but the weekly long trips had taken a toll on him. Alan had spoken to Mr. Stockburn about leaving the coal mining business and starting to live off his land for a while. He had been dealing with buying and selling beef cattle for a few years on a small scale with Yano and Koda doing most of the work, but he was thinking about growing that a little larger and expanding his pastureland to hold more cattle. He, also, would like to work part time at the sawmill. Sawmill lumber was in big demand with all the building that was taking place in Shepherd Springs, and Alan loved building things. Alan told Mr. Stockburn how much he had enjoyed his job and how thankful he was to him for hiring him seventeen years ago, but thought it was time to move on now. Mr. Stockburn understood and appreciated the good job he had done for the company, but, most of all, he was honored to call him friend and told Alan if he ever needed anything to let him know. Alan told Mr. Stockburn he planned to stay until the end of August to help John Thomas and Jacob Bolin get the new section opened and operating. That was great news for Mr. Stockburn because he needed Alan's help, and he could not thank him enough for his willingness to oversee the mine to make sure it was up and operating as normal without any problems. He knew he could offer Alan more money to stay on with him, but he, also, understood Alan and knew he would not accept the offer. That was not Alan's character and that was another thing he admired about him. They shook hands and agreed to stay in touch. Mr. Stockburn told him not to be surprised if he called on him from time to time for advice. Alan assured him that he could call him anytime and he would do anything he could to help him.

Yano was sixteen now and no longer in school. He spent a lot of his time tending to their cattle with the twins' help when they were not in school. He still goes on his adventures by himself, when he can and sometimes takes Nokomis, Ayita and Koda with him to the cabin at the lake. He would always listen and watch on every trip to the cabin, but he had never heard the howling of the Wolf or seen any Wolf pups when his siblings were with him. Yano knew now that, so far, he had only seen the Spirit of the Wolf when he was by himself.

When Sloppy was staying with them in the shanty, Yano tried to spend as much time as he could with him. He had much to learn from Sloppy about survival in the mountains for so many years. Sloppy, even up in years, helped with the chores, cutting firewood, tending livestock and riding into town for supplies. Although the Adams didn't expect it, it was his way of doing his part while he stayed at the Adams' homeplace. They knew Sloppy and he would not have it any other way. Alan had learned so much about him in the past seventeen years. He had some secrets that he had never told Sloppy, and he was absolutely sure that Sloppy had many secrets, also, that were unknown to him or anyone. They were good friends and would always be, with a bond of trust between them, but some secrets were not to be shared by either.

Chapter 2

There had been many changes from 1860 to 1865. Abraham Lincoln was elected the 16th President of the United States. A Civil War began April 12, 1861, when the Confederates bombarded Union Soldiers at Fort Sumter, South Carolina. The four reasons for the start of the war were the disagreements over slavery, States vs Federal rights, the election of President Abraham Lincoln and the economy. The war was known as the war between the states, the Union against the Confederates, the war between the Northern and Southern States, the Yankees against the Rebels, or the Blue-Gray War. In 1861, the State of Virginia was a Confederate State. The people in Virginia were considered to be in the Confederacy until 1863 when western Virginia became a separate state from Virginia and would be known as West Virginia and would be a Union State. January 1, 1863, President Lincoln issued the Emancipation Proclamation. The proclamation declared that all persons held as slaves were to be freed. Alan had lived in that region of Virginia his whole life and even though it was considered a

Confederate state, he remained neutral in that war, mostly because of his and his wife's Indian ancestry. They had seen Union troops traveling on Three Bears Trail and Confederate troops traveling through Shepherd Springs. Sometimes they could hear the blast of the cannons as they did battle two miles away down on the Potomac River. The war ended April 9, 1865, when Robert E. Lee surrendered the last major Confederate Army to Ulysses S. Grant at Appomattox Courthouse in Virginia.

Alan Adams never understood the war or why so many soldiers had to die. April 15, 1865, President Abraham Lincoln was assassinated by John Wilkes Booth at the Ford Theater in Washington, D.C. Booth was twenty-six years old when he assassinated President Lincoln. Twelve days after the assassination, Booth was found hiding in a tobacco barn in Virginia and died in a gun battle. Andrew Johnson was Vice President at the time, and he became the 17th President of the United States.

Yano and Alan had spent time doing a little prospecting at the cabin at the lake for the last three years. They found enough gold to purchase more land. It was a dream come true, but before arranging a meeting with a land agent, Alan talked with Odina and filled her in on the two tracts of land he wanted to purchase. They both agreed it would be good for their family and future, so Alan made plans to contact the Federal Land Agent, Robert Perry. After talking with Mr. Perry, they set up a meeting to discuss the two tracts Alan wanted to buy. The six-hundred-acre tract joined his northern tract, and another four-hundred-acre tract joined his southern tract. Mr. Perry had the land surveyed; they agreed on the purchase price and the deal was complete, the Adams now owned a total of two thousand acres of land which had plenty of gold on it that nobody knew about.

Alan and Yano were enjoying exploring the new land they now owned and were excited to find another lake on the north end of it. There was a large creek that fed the lake that looked to be as deep as the lake at the cabin. It looked like it also had some good fishing holes. The creek ran southwest through the new property, eventually crossing Three Bears Trail close to their western property line. Yano was already thinking of building another cabin on the new land at the north end close to the creek and

Three Bears Trail. On the south end, they had started adding more pasture by fencing in a large section for more grazing space for their cattle.

Chapter 3

It had now been two days since the twin's birthday and Sloppy had his supplies loaded on his pack mule. Before leaving, he told Yano he had more clues he wanted to leave for him that would help him find his hidden treasures when the time came. This worried Yano because he felt that Sloppy was thinking more about his age and his upcoming death. Sloppy said his goodbyes to the Adams' family and started on his two-day journey to his home in the Appalachian Mountains. Yano watched as he rode off thinking he looked healthy, but he also knew he could not do what he used to do and hoped to see him ride back to their home in two weeks as always.

Yano thought to himself, he should check on Sloppy before his normal stay of two weeks was up, but Sloppy loved the mountain life at his place and he would never want to intrude on his privacy. He knew Sloppy carried enough food supplies to last longer than two weeks, but if he did not see him riding up in two weeks, he would begin the trip to make sure he was okay. With Sloppy getting older, he only stayed gone now for two weeks at a time. He did not want to admit that he did not have the strength he once had to handle all the many dangers of the rugged mountains he called home.

As Sloppy headed north on Three Bears Trail, he crossed the creek that ran down through the north end of the new property the Adams had purchased. He could see four Confederate soldiers approaching and wondered if they knew the war was over. He sat still on his horse and as they got closer, he could tell they were tired, hungry, and heading home. "You soldiers know the war is over don't you?" said Sloppy.

"Yes, we know," one of the soldiers replied, "we are just trying to get home to North Carolina." They told Sloppy they had been trying to get home for over a month, avoiding several Union troops they ran across along the way that may not know the war was over. One of the soldiers said they had not eaten in a few days and would like to water their horses and fill their canteens at the creek, if he didn't mind.

Without saying a word, while they were watering their horses and filling up their canteens, Sloppy got off his horse and started gathering up a bag of food for the soldiers from his pack mule. He could tell one of the soldiers was keeping an eye on him and finally got around to asking if he was from a Confederate State or Union State.

Sloppy said, "I'm 73 years old and I've lived in this region of the Appalachian Mountains most of my life." He went on to tell them, "until 1863 this area was known as the Confederate State of Virginia, then in 1863 the government cut a line through the northwestern section of Virginia and called it West Virginia, a Union State." He said, "I've stayed completely neutral in this war, but I would have defended my friends and property against either side." He then handed them enough food to last a few days.

They were so thankful for the food and asked Sloppy how far it was to Shepherd Springs from where they were. They said they were hoping to be able to catch a train there and get home to North Carolina.

He told them it was about four miles, to just keep going south on Three Bears Trail.

The soldier then asked if he thought the railroad people would give four worn out soldiers with four worn out horses a free ride because they had no money to purchase tickets.

Sloppy said, "I don't know if they will do that or not." Without saying anything else, he lifted the flap of his saddlebag, retrieved a small cloth tobacco pouch and handed it to the soldier. Sloppy told them to take the pouch to the Trading Post in Shepherd Springs and see Beanstalk. "He is tall and when you meet him, you will see why everybody calls him Beanstalk. He will buy this gold, there's about three ounces there and that should pay for your train ride home with enough left for something to eat."

All the soldiers looked at Sloppy in amazement and thanked him over and over for his kindness, but they could not help, but ask why he would help four old tired and worn-out soldiers that were complete strangers.

Sloppy looked at the soldiers and told them to sit down by the creek, relax and dig out some of the food he gave them and listen. He said, "It's true, I do not know you, but you are not strangers to me because I know what you have been through and what you have seen in the war. I see it in your eyes. You fought for a cause you thought was right and I thank you. This little bit of food and gold that I have given you does not compare to what y'all have given." Sloppy asked for their names and Ned was the first to speak, then Bill, Theo and Ezekiel. "It was nice to meet you brave men, they just call me Sloppy and all that I ask is, if you run across someone in need of help, then help them if you can. Now, I have two days of riding to get where I am going so, I need to ride on."

The soldiers thanked Sloppy again for his help, they knew, because of him, they would now make it home. As they rested at the creek, eating deer jerky and flatbread, they watched Sloppy till he was completely out of sight, riding north on Three Bears Trail.

Chapter 4

Sloppy arrived at his halfway camp just before dark and took a much-needed rest. He was feeling good about helping the four soldiers and sure hoped they would make it home okay. He ate a piece of deer jerky with flatbread, rolled out his bedroll under the little lean to that he could sleep in and while thinking about his day, drifted off to sleep.

Sloppy arrived at his cabin at noon the next day. He unloaded his remaining supplies from his mule, then removed the saddle from his horse and put them both in the coral. While doing an inventory of his food supplies, he noticed that there was not enough for two weeks stay like he had planned, so he would cut his time short. Sloppy built a fire in the wood stove so he could make a pot of coffee. Once the coffee was made, he sat at the table with paper and pencil and began to write. The first thing he wrote was a letter stating that at the time of his death, he wished to leave his eight hundred acres of land and the cabin with all his belongings to Yano Adams. He put the date on the letter and signed it. Next, he drew a plat map of his land and put an X mark at a few locations on the map. This was how his best friend, Fred Smith, had done it. It would be up to Yano to find these locations. He wrote some more clues on another piece of paper and tomorrow, would place all of the notes at the first location that he told Yano to find.

Sloppy decided he wanted fish for supper this evening, so he got his fishing pole and went to his little fishing hole to catch supper. This fishing hole was about two hundred yards behind his cabin and was on the same creek that ran alongside the path to his cabin. There was also a small waterfall that came out of the side of the mountain and dumped into this pool of water. Where the water came out of the mountain, there was a small opening that looked like it might go back into the mountain a little ways. Sloppy had explored this opening many times. The first time he crawled through it, he found that it opened up large enough for him to stand up. He made some torches for light and discovered the cave goes back into the mountain about a hundred feet where he found many treasures of gemstones and gold. He had this location marked on his notes for Yano to find. Sloppy was able to catch two perch and that would be enough for supper. He sat on a large boulder at the edge of the fishing hole and enjoyed the sounds and smells of the mountains that he called home. Many different locations on his land were his happy places and this was one of them.

It was warm in the Appalachian Mountains in July, but as the evening came, it's nice with a little mountain breeze blowing down through the mountains. Sloppy had a good meal of fried fish and potatoes and now he was sitting on his porch drinking coffee with a smile on his face, listening to the sounds that had pleased him for over forty years. At seventy-three years old, Sloppy knew he had more years behind him than in front of him, but tonight, everything was right in his world.

There was something special about sitting on a porch. It was a great place to just relax and think, tonight Sloppy was remembering his journey of life. Sloppy was born in 1792, his mother died in 1800. At eight years old, his father taught him how to trap, hunt for food and how to prospect for gold and precious gemstones to sell or trade. Sloppy's father died in 1815. He already knew how to survive in the mountains, but decided to try coal mining. Sloppy was never afraid of hard work and was proud of the little pay he got. After three years of working in the coal mines, he left and went to work at a sawmill, where he worked for two years. At twenty-eight years old, he decided that he wanted to be a mountain man and live on his own land. Sloppy had some money saved up from selling his pelts and selling gold and gemstones that he had prospected, along with the money he was paid for working in the coal mines and sawmill. He was able to purchase this eight-hundred-acre tract of land from the government that was really hard to get to, but that's what he liked. His father had always told him that gold could be found even though it was not known for large veins of gold to be in this mountain region, you just have to know what to look for.

He was remembering how he was able to sell the pelts of the wild game he had trapped on his land and the long trips into town to sell his goods. Most of all, he remembered when he met what would become his best friend, Fred Smith. They hunted, fished and trapped together. They even helped each other when building their cabins. Sloppy missed his old friend, but he was thankful for his new friends, Alan, Odina, Yano, Ayita, Koda and Nokomis Adams.

Sloppy got up from his chair on the porch and stepped up to a porch post and stared out into the darkness when he heard the eerie scream of a mountain lion off in the distance. He recognized the sound and thought it was a female lion that he had named Isabell. He had seen and heard her many times and it sounded like she was on top of the mountain where the chair tree was. Exactly where he would go tomorrow to hide the notes that he wanted Yano to find.

Chapter 5

Sloppy was feeling tired, but good, as he was lying in his bed, waiting for sleep to come. He was happy that he could help those four Confederate soldiers, even though it would cut his time short that he was planning on staying at his place. He had a secret place to pan for gold and would go there before he went back to the Adams.

Now, daylight was making its way down in the valleys of the mountains as Sloppy awoke from a restful sleep. He built a fire in the wood stove, so he could make a pot of coffee. Once the coffee was ready, he poured himself a cup and sat on the porch to watch the morning come to life. After thirty or forty minutes, he went back in to cook a little breakfast.

Old Chester was saddled up. Sloppy would carry a long rope, his pan for panning gold, a canteen of water and some deer jerky to eat should he get hungry. He rode down the path for about a half of a mile until he got to the chair tree. He rode Chester across the creek and over a small hill that was in line with the area that he would need to be at. After tying Chester to a tree at the base of the mountain, he gathered the rope and started his climb. At seventy-three years old, climbing up that mountain was getting more difficult. He had done it a couple of times since he fell and broke his leg a few years ago. He started his climb slowly and carefully, being alert for that mountain lion that frequents the area. After reaching the top, he carefully looped his rope around a tree and tied the ends together and threw the tied end over the side of the mountain. He did it that way, so when he got to the bottom, he could untie the ends and just pull his rope down. Sloppy was able to hide his notes in a secure spot. He was relieved that this detail was complete because he knew he probably would not be climbing up here again. He had a few more hiding places closer to the ground and they were marked on the map for Yano to find. Using the rope, he climbed down the mountain now, hoping his hands were strong enough to keep a good grip on the rope. He made it down with no problems this time.

Riding Chester down through this valley, he went to a little branch where he had found gold before and would pan for gold there. This was another secret spot, but probably not as good as the one he would go to later or tomorrow. He hoped he could find three or four ounces to carry back with him. When he got to the spot, he got the pan and a small shovel out that was tied on the back of the saddle and went to work. He had a couple of empty tobacco pouches in his pocket to put the gold in that he expected to find. He found more than two ounces of gold at this spot in a little over two hours. He stopped prospecting and would fix it back to look normal, as if nobody had been digging there. Taking a break sitting against a tree, he ate some deer jerky and drank water. After relaxing for a few minutes, he struggled to get up on his feet, but he managed to get on his horse and headed back to the cabin. Now, he had been sitting on his porch with a cup of coffee on his mind.

After he had rested a little and had his coffee, he knew he needed to cut some more firewood for the wood stove. He always tried to replace the amount of wood he used as soon as he could. Sloppy was too tired to go to the other secret spot for panning gold. He had worked so much in the heat today, he decided to go to the fishing hole and take a bath and just soak in the cool water. He grabbed a bar of lye soap, a change of clothes and walked back to the fishing hole. Downstream a few feet from the fishing hole was a hole of water deep enough for him to bathe in. There were some large flat rocks that he could lay on to let the sun and warm weather dry him and his clothes that he would wash too. The coolness of the water had perked him up a little, but he wouldn't go to the other secret gold panning site until tomorrow. Its location was on the other end of his land. The rest of the day, he would rest and piddle around the cabin.

He was up before daylight the next morning having his coffee while sitting on the porch. He wanted to get an early start and hoped to find a few more ounces of gold. Sloppy had enough gold and gemstone hidden away to buy himself a large plantation somewhere or anything else he desired, but he didn't want anything other than what he had now.

On his ride to the secret gold panning site, Sloppy saw a black bear with two cubs up ahead of him. The cubs were playing, climbing trees and running back and forth to each other as the sow kept watch on her young. Sloppy knew not to get in between the sow and her cubs and they were playing right on the trail he needed to travel. He just sat still on his horse and watched them for a few minutes, then they wandered off, so he could continue on his way. He never got tired of seeing the wildlife on his land.

When he reached his secret spot, he grabbed his short handle shovel, his pan and this time, he brought a sifting screen that was about one foot square in size. He scooped up a shovel full and dumped it in the sifting screen with the pan under it. The screen would hold the bigger pebbles and he would inspect each one before he dumped them off to the side. His first shovel had some small nuggets and a lot of flakes. He carefully removed the gold and put it in a tobacco pouch. The next four shovels produced only a few flakes. He knew to dig deeper and when he did, he picked up more nuggets, bigger than the first ones. Sloppy took a break, sat on the hill above the ditch where the treasure was and drank some water and ate some deer jerky. He could feel something watching him and turned to his left to see a large black bear thirty yards away staring at him. It was not the sow with cubs he had seen earlier, it was a large boar, probably four hundred pounds and it seemed the bear wanted some of his deer jerky. Sloppy had his forty-five Colt Revolver and his knife on his side, but that fifty caliber Hawking Rifle would be better if he needed to shoot the bear, but it was ten yards away in the scabbard on his horse. He preferred not to shoot the bear, but it was approaching him. He drew his revolver as he stood up and threw his hands up in the air, then yelled at the bear. When the bear was about ten yards away, Sloppy fired his gun into the ground in front of the bear. That worked, the bear turned and ran off.

Sloppy had worked enough today and found about four or five ounces of gold, plus the excitement of being face to face with a four-hundred-pound bear. He decided to head back to the cabin. Since he was low on food, he would head back to the Adams in the morning and would arrive a few days earlier than they expected him to.

Chapter 6

Sitting on his porch drinking coffee, Sloppy was reminiscing about living and surviving in these Appalachian Mountains for the last forty-five years. He remembered how happy this life made him. He wrote a few more notes that he would leave in the cabin for Yano to find. He wrote about how he named the female mountain lion Isabell and to be careful when she came around. Also, he talked about the four-hundred-pound black bear that could be aggressive and cause him harm. He wrote about good locations to trap and what to trap at those locations. He wouldn't leave any information about the gold and gemstones in the cabin, all of that information was written down on the notes he had hidden for Yano to find. Being secretive is still his way of life. Sloppy was confident that Yano would find his treasures after he died.

He planned to leave early in the morning to go back to the Adams' homestead. He drank his last sip of coffee and went into the cabin to go to sleep. He knew he could stay longer and not go hungry, but he missed his friends that have become family. He didn't understand these feelings he had about people now, when all of his life, he was happy to be alone, but he was older now and not able to do what he loved doing and had come to love his friends more.

He was up at daybreak; the first order of business was to make coffee and cook up a little breakfast, then he would bag up all the remaining food supplies to carry back with him. Once he had saddled up Chester and tied everything else on the mule to haul, he started his two-day journey back. The weather was nice today, a little warm, but no chance of rain. He rode past his halfway camp and decided to go a few miles further before bedding down for the night. Sloppy rode on up to a little spot next to a creek where he had camped before. He was pretty tired now, so he would bed down there and would not have far to go to reach his shanty at the Adams' homestead tomorrow.

When he woke up the next morning, he had a hard time getting up off the ground. His leg and back hurt after sleeping on the hard ground all night. Once he was able to stand upright and move around a little, he stoked up the fire to make a pot of coffee. With his coffee, he would have a couple of pieces of bacon and a corn fritter that he had wrapped up in a cloth in his saddlebag.

After breakfast and coffee, Sloppy saddled up Chester and loaded the remaining supplies back on his mule. He took a big ole chew of tobacco and started his ride back again. He should get there around lunchtime and would be glad to see his friends. After two hours of riding, he reached Three Bears Trail and headed south. As he approached the creek that crosses Three Bears Trail, he could see a wagon stopped there, letting two mules get water. As he got closer, he could see that the people on the wagon were Negros. Sloppy said, "Howdy folks."

The older man hopped off the wagon, removed his ole floppy hat, bowed his head down and said, "Hey Masser, we ain't meaning no harm, jus letting our mules get some water from this here creek. Wee's been coming a long way and it's been hot and dusty."

Sloppy said, "first thing is, I'm not no master, you can call me Sloppy."

The older man said, "Yes sur, Mr. Sloppy, I'm Henry Cole, that there woman is Eliza Cole and our children Tom and Fanny. We'd be freed now and jus traveling to find work and make a better life. After we be freed, Masser Cox say we can stay on his farm and work and do a little share cropping and help with the other work and he would make sure wees had food to eat and a roof over our head, but he couldn't pay us money. Wees had nowhere to go, so we stayed. Then Masser Cox died, and Ms. Cox sold the farm, so wees had to leave. Even doe wees be freed, it was jus like wees wasn't."

Sloppy asked, "What kind of work can you do?"

Henry said, "Me Masser had me tending cattle and chickens, working at his sawmill and farming corn, peas, potatoes and onions. I's can do most any kind of work and so can my son Tom. Masser Cox really like onions and Eliza would use them when cooking meals for them."

Sloppy asked if they had any food with them.

Henry said, "Naw Sir, we ran out the other day."

Sloppy hopped off his horse and went to his mule and untied what was left of his food supply and said, "here, take this and see if you can use it?"

Their sad look on their faces turned into smiles and Sloppy knew he had done something good for those folks.

Henry asked Sloppy, if he knew of any work where a Negro would bees hired.

Sloppy said, "No I don't right now, but you could check in Shepherd Springs, which is four miles from here. There is a sawmill and a grist mill on the back side of town on the Red Wolf River that might hire you and your boy. There is a livery stable at the end of town, you might check there too."

"Thanks, you Mr. Sloppy, wees sho will check on that, but first wees gonna pull off this path and cook up some of this here food yous done gave us."

Sloppy really wanted to help this family and was thinking about something that would help them and Alan too, but he would need to talk to Alan before saying anything to Henry Cole. He asked Henry if he had any money to buy more food with.

Henry replied, "Naw Sir, not till I gets a paying job. My children, Tom is fifteen and a hards worker and Fanny is twelve and cans works hard too."

Sloppy wanted to do more for this family, so he went over to his saddlebags and pulled out a tobacco pouch that had about three ounces of gold in it and gave it to Henry.

"Mr. Sloppy, what is this that you gives me?"

"It's gold Henry, take it to the Trading Post in Shepherd Springs and see a tall man that goes by the name of Beanstalk, and he will buy it from you."

"Okay, Mr. Sloppy, then I's brings the moneys to you, but how do I's finds you?"

"No, you keep it to buy food or whatever you need, I just want to help your family a little."

"I's thanks you Mr. Sloppy, ain't nobody ever dones sumthang like this for us."

Sloppy said, "I have to go now Henry, you take care of your family and I'll probably see you again soon."

Chapter 7

Sloppy rode up the path to his shanty. Yano saw him and thought something was wrong because he was a few days early, so he ran down to meet him. The other kids came running too, they were glad to see him. Alan and Odina came out of their cabin and walked down to the shanty to check on Sloppy.

He could see the worried look on everyone's face and he told them he was alright, just came back a few days early because he was running a little low on food.

Alan said, "Sloppy you carried enough food for more than two weeks. Did you get injured or sick and is that the reason you came back early?"

Sloppy said, "No, it was nothing like that. I gave some food supplies to some people that really needed it and that caused me to be a little short on supplies, so I just came back early."

Alan told Yano and Koda to take care of Sloppy's horse and mule, he could tell Sloppy wanted to talk with him alone.

Sloppy hugged Ayita, Nokomis and Odina and assured them that he was fine, then all the girls went back to the cabin, leaving Sloppy and Alan there to talk.

Sloppy began to tell Alan about his trip. He said when he left, he came upon four Confederate soldiers at the creek that crosses Three Bears Trail about one mile north of here. The soldiers looked worn out and hungry. They had traveled a long way and were trying to get to Shepherd Springs to hopefully catch a train ride down to North Carolina, closer to where they were from. They told me they had no money and asked if I thought they would give four ole worn out soldiers and their horses a free train ride. "I told them I didn't know if they would do that or not. I gave them a good amount of my food, so they would have something to eat, knowing it would cut my time down at staying at my place, but I felt good doing that. I, then handed one of them a cloth tobacco pouch with about three ounces of gold in it and told them they could pay for their train ride with that, but first go to the Trading Post and see Beanstalk, he would purchase it and there should be extra for something to eat. They were grateful for the help and promised to make it up to me if they ran into me again. I told them not to worry about paying me back, y'all have done enough, seen enough and sacrificed enough, just get to your homes safely and rest, the war is over."

Alan said he saw those four Confederate soldiers when they rode by, headed to Shepherd Springs. "I hope they made it home; you did a good thing Sloppy, and we are glad you came back early."

Sloppy said, "I was able to catch fish to eat, sit on my porch and drink coffee, did a little panning for gold and took a long and much needed bath in the cool creek. Those few days I stayed there did me a lot of good and it was no problem to come back early. On my return trip back, when I approached that same creek that crosses Three Bears Trail, I noticed a wagon at the creek. There were four Negros on that wagon, they were letting their mules get water from the creek. They looked scared to death when I rode up to them and quickly announced to me that they were now freed and were looking for work to build a better life. I talked with this family for a while and learned a lot about them. They were hungry and tired, so I gave them the rest of my food supplies and about three ounces of gold to sell to Beanstalk. Henry Cole is the father; Eliza is his wife and the mother of their children. Their son, Tom Cole, is fifteen and daughter, Fanny Cole, is twelve. I asked Henry what kind of work he did when he was owned as a slave. Henry said he tended to the cattle, chickens, farmed the land to raise corn, peas and onions. He also worked at the owner's sawmill. He claims he can do any kind of work."

Alan said, "Sloppy, you have a giver's heart and love helping people out during their hardships of life and that's another thing we admire about you. I have witnessed you doing the same thing many times. Sloppy, you are holding something back, like you want to say more about this family."

"Well, I guess I do. If Henry can or can't get a job in town, they will still live out of their wagon and may not have food to eat. I was thinking if you are serious about raising more cattle, Henry and his son Tom, might be a good hand to help out. I know I have no right to even talk about this because it's your land, but it may be a good deal for both of you. We could build them a suitable dwelling on the south end of your land where the cattle will be. They are not educated people, but I can tell they are good people that are willing to work hard. If things didn't work out, it will still be your land and house that we build."

Alan said, "let's saddle up a couple horses and ride to the south end to look around. if you feel up to it."

Sloppy smiled and said, "I'm up to it."

Alan was thinking this might not be a bad idea, but he would talk to Odina first and wait to meet this family.

As they were riding through the south end of the property, Alan saw the perfect spot to build a house. It had a flat piece of ground with water close by and easy access, so a wagon could haul the lumber needed to build the house. Sloppy watched Alan as he surveyed the area, and he could tell that he was interested in his suggestion.

Alan could tell Sloppy was tired, so he said, "let's go back and have some supper and let me sleep on this. If we decide to give this family a try, could you locate them again?"

Sloppy said, "I think I can, Henry was going to check in town for a job at the livery stable or the sawmill. I know they will be living out of their wagon, probably on the outskirts of town."

"Okay," Alan said, "we'll talk more in the morning."

Odina had supper ready when they got back. Alan told Yano and Koda to take care of the horses and then come to supper. After a fine meal, Sloppy went to his shanty to drink some coffee while sitting on his porch before he turned in for the night.

Alan was talking to Odina about what he and Sloppy were thinking about doing and hiring this Negro family to help with the chores of raising more cattle. He told her that this family had left the farm where they stayed after they were freed because the owner died, and the woman sold the farm. They were looking to make a better life for themselves, and this could be good for them and us, also.

Odina looked at Alan with a proud smile and said, "I believe we can help this family."

Alan said, "I do too, but I really want us to meet them first. We will need to build a house for them to stay in and I have picked out a place to do just that. Down on the south end of the property is the perfect spot. I trust Sloppy's judgment of people's character, and he feels good about helping this family. He had not said anything to them, he wanted to talk to me first. I told him to let me sleep on it and talk to you and would let him know in the morning. In a few weeks, I'll be leaving my coal mining job and will be at home with you and the kids and we could use the help raising more cattle. We will have to spend more money to get started, but I feel it will pay off in the long run."

Sloppy was tired as he laid in his bed, but sleep didn't come. He was thinking about the four Confederate soldiers and wondering if they made it home. He was also thinking about that Negro family, hoping that Alan thought it was a good idea and hired them. He would feel responsible if it didn't work out.

Chapter 8

Odina was up early, making biscuits, bacon and coffee. Alan poured himself a cup of coffee and went to sit on the porch while waiting for the biscuits to be done. He could see smoke coming from the flu down at Sloppy's shanty. Sloppy was up and making coffee. Alan planned to walk down there with a couple of bacon and biscuits when they were done.

Alan had thought about hiring this Negro family most of the night. Alan and Odina both have such a giving heart and love helping people in need. He knew to be cautious until he knew this family, but he trusted Sloppy's judgment on their character. He walked down to Sloppy's shanty with a couple of bacon biscuits to tell him of his decision. Alan told Sloppy he would like to meet this family; he had talked it over with Odina and decided that they would help this family, and they could help us with the work around here.

Sloppy smiled and said, "I think you will be glad to have the help, and I think this family will do a good job at whatever their job is."

Alan said, "I know we can provide food to them, so they won't go hungry and pay a little at first for the work they do. See if you can find them and ask if they are interested. If he didn't get a job in town, I will be interested in talking to him."

Sloppy said he needed to go to town for some supplies and he would find them if they were still there.

Alan saddled up his and Sloppy's horse. When Sloppy headed into town, he would ride over the south property some more to make sure he had picked the best spot to build another dwelling on his property. If the Negro family took what he offered, this would be their home to live in as long as they stayed here and worked.

When Sloppy got into town, his first stop was the Trading Post. He had a few ounces of gold to sell. He asked Beanstalk if a Negro family came in yesterday to sell some gold.

Beanstalk said, "Sure did, a little over three ounces and I gave them fifty-six dollars for it. They were a pitiful looking bunch, uneducated, but very polite."

Sloppy said, "Yes, they are. I gave them the gold to help them buy food. Their last name is Cole and the man,

Henry, is looking for work. Do you know where they are now?"

"The first place they went was to the General Store next door, then I watched them go toward the livery stable."

"Okay, thanks, now see what you will give me for these few ounces of gold?"

Beanstalk weighed the gold and said, "it's a little over four ounces, I'll give you seventy-five dollars for it."

"Sounds good, thanks," said Sloppy." Sloppy left and went to the General Store next door, got his supplies, then headed down to the livery stable. He asked Jacob Jenkins if a Negro man asked for a job there yesterday.

Jacob said, "Yes, he did, but I couldn't hire him, my brother and I are all we need right now."

"Do you know where he went from here?"

"Well, he said he was going to check at the sawmill and gristmill for work, so he headed that way I believe." said Jacob."

Sloppy left the livery stable looking for the Coles. Before he got to the sawmill on the Red Wolf River, he spotted their wagon back off the trail where they had camped. As he rode up to their wagon, he saw Eliza cooking over an open fire. They were frightened when he first rode up, then they recognized him and got the biggest smile on their faces.

Henry said, "Well hello Misser Sloppy, shows is good to sees you sir."

Sloppy asked Henry if he had got a job yet. "Naw sir, the livery stable said naw, the sawmill said naw and the gristmill said naw, but I's keeps looking sir."

"Well, I have something if you would be interested."

"Yes sir, I's interested."

Sloppy said, "a good friend of mine raises cattle and needs someone to help tend the cattle, put up more fencing and some of the land is farmable to raise crops on. You and your family could set up a camp there and if it works out, he said he would build a house for you to stay in. My friend's name is Alan Adams. He lives there with his wife Odina and four children, Yano is sixteen, the twins, Ayita and Koda are twelve and their youngest Nokomis is ten. Alan wants to talk to you if you are interested. They live three miles north of here on Three Bears Trail, the same trail that brought you to Shepherd

Springs. If you are interested, I'll ride out there with you,"

"I stay with them for months at a time. Mr. Sloppy, I's sho is interested and can be ready to go in a few minutes."

Sloppy said, "Alan will be able to pay you a little for the work you do and will supply your family with food, so you won't go hungry. Take your time in loading up, because I'm going to the other end of town and will meet you at Three Bears Trail in thirty or forty minutes. Just wait for me there and I will ride in with you."

"Yessur, we sho will waits for you there."

Sloppy was going to Roosters Tavern for a quick drink and would always buy a bottle of whiskey to take with him.

Chapter 9

Henry was nervous about meeting the Adams. He had been told no so many times before. With Sloppy leading the way, the Coles pulled their wagon up to the front porch of the Adams' house. Alan and Odina stepped out on the porch and said, "Howdy folks."

Henry hopped down from the wagon, removed his ole floppy hat, lowered his head and said, "Hey Misser Adams."

Alan said, "My name is Alan, this is my wife Odina and that young man walking up is Yano, he is our oldest at sixteen, we have three more around back, probably playing."

Henry said, "This here woman is Eliza, our son Tom, he's fifteen and our daughter Fanny, she is twelve."

Alan said, "pleased to meet you folks."

Odina spoke up and asked if she could get them something to drink, cool water or a cup of sassafras tea she had just made.

They said, "nos thank you mam."

Alan said, "here's our other three children coming around to the front of the house. Those two up front are our twins, Ayita and Koda, they are twelve years old like your daughter and the little one behind them is Nokomis, she's ten."

Yano looked at Tom and asked if he would like to go to the barn and see their horses. Tom hopped out of the wagon and said, I guess, and they left walking to the barn. Ayita saw Fanny still sitting in the wagon and asked her if she would want to swing on their swing. Fanny said, "okay," and hopped out of the wagon.

Henry said, "That's the first time Is had seen a smile on my children's faces in a long time."

Odina invited Eliza to get out of the wagon and come inside so the men could talk. Eliza was reluctant at first, but, then in a noticeable shyness said, "Yes mam", and went into the cabin with Odina.

Odina said, "please call me Odina,"

Eliza smiled and said, "Okay, Odina."

Alan said, "Sloppy told me that you were looking for work."

"Yessur Mr. Adams, jus trying to makes a better life for my wife and chilrens."

Alan said he would like to talk to him about helping with cattle and a little farming, I am planning on getting more cattle and would need some help doing other things around the place. "What kind of work have you done before?"

Henry said he tended cattle, chickens, hogs, did some building of barns, sheds and lots of farming, plowing the land, planting the seed and gathering the crops. "I digs lots of wells too."

Alan said, "you sound like someone I need to help here. Here's what I can offer. I have a spot on the south end of the property that has water and a good spot to camp. We will help build a temporary structure for y'all to stay in until we can build a more suitable dwelling that you and your family can live in. I need more fences to be put up, so I can have more cattle. I will supply all the material needed for the fence and buildings, but I will need your help with the labor. I will feed you and your family until you get on your feet and pay you two dollars a week at first. When we start selling cattle, hogs, eggs or crops that are harvested here, you will get a portion of that money too.”

“I’s thanks you Mr. Adams, I’s will works hard for you. My boy can works hard too. My wife and daughter knows how to farm and will be a big help when planting season is here.”

Alan called for Yano. When he came, Alan told him to hook up the mule to the large wagon and load up those large canvas tarps that were in the loft, then ten of those poles that were behind the barn. “Next, I want you to go to the stack of lumber over there and load about fifteen pieces eight and six feet long. Be sure to bring nails, hammers, a saw and a shovel. When you get all of that loaded up, follow our tracks to the south end. Koda, you help him load that stuff and ride with him to the south end.”

Henry told his son Tom to help Yano load that stuff up too. While the boys were busy loading up the wagon, Alan told Henry there were a few things that he required of him. He said, “never steal from me, never lie to me, be honest, if you need something, just ask and respect the people, the land and the wildlife.”

Henry said, "Yesser you have my word."

Odina and Eliza had learned a lot about each other and had become friends. The kids had become friends already and Alan had gained employees that will become friends.

Henry was thinking a better life for his family had started when they arrived at the spot that they would call home. Alan showed Henry the spot where he wanted to build a house, so don't build anything on that spot. They continued to walk around the section of land while Eliza and Fanny set up their camp. Alan showed Henry a gate on the back fence line where he could put his two mules in the pasture with the cattle, so they could graze and get water. Henry's wagon was covered, and his wife and daughter usually slept in it and he and Tom slept on the ground under a tarp.

Yano arrived with the wagon loaded with the material, so they could set up a tent that would serve as a temporary shelter. Alan, Henry, Yano, Koda and Tom got the wood poles set for the frame of the tent, then draped the tarps over it to make a shelter. Alan told Henry to just work around there today and tomorrow to make and build the things he needed with the lumber they brought, and he would check on them tomorrow. He asked if they had food to eat tonight and tomorrow morning.

Henry said, "Yes sir, thanks to Misser Sloppy, he helps us a lot."

Alan, Yano and Koda returned home feeling good that they helped the Coles. Odina told of her talk with Eliza. She said, "their children can't read or write and Henry and Eliza can only write their name. This got me to thinking, I could teach them to read and write here because I know Negros are not allowed to go to school with white children."

Alan smiled at his wife's beautiful heart, and he knew she would have them reading and writing in no time. He asked Odina what she thought about him cashing in some of the gold, so he could pay for the lumber to build a suitable dwelling for the Coles. He said, "we would have to spend money to make money later."

Odina replied, "I think we should and in a few more weeks, you'll be through with your trips to Rockford and can concentrate on working your own land like you have always dreamed of."

Alan drew up some plans for the house he wanted to build there and started making a list of the material he would need. He was getting excited, he really loved building things. Alan told Odina that he would ask Clyde Bolin if he and his son, Lucas, would help build the house. He said it would not take long to build if he, Yano, Koda, Henry, Tom, Clyde and Lucas did the building with Sloppy supervising and making trips to the sawmill to haul the lumber back to us.

After a good supper, Alan and Odina went to sit on the porch, he had a cup of coffee, and both were sitting in rocking chairs thinking and planning. When they went to bed, they were happy and excited to help this family and fell asleep with a smile on their face.

Chapter 10

Sloppy wasn't sure what Alan would think of his suggestion of hiring the Negro family. He knew it would be an expense for him to start with, but was pleased to see him excited about it and already making plans to make it work for everybody. Sloppy had some secrets too, about what he could do to help finance this family to get a new start on a better life. Not only did he have a lot of gold hidden at his place in the Appalachian Mountains, but he also had a pretty good stash of gold and money hidden inside his shanty and always carried a few ounces of gold in his saddlebags. Sloppy felt responsible for the expense of hiring this family because it was his suggestion that got it started. He intended to use his money and gold to pay for the building supplies and supplies the family needed to get started. Alan didn't know this yet and had already made plans to cash in some of their gold to pay for it.

It was Sunday morning, as the rooster crowed. Alan was up before daylight, making his coffee and sitting at the table, adding to his list of lumber he would need for the house. He had to catch the train to Rockford the next morning and would be gone for three days, so he would get Yano and Sloppy to go to the sawmill and give the lumber order to the Morris brothers and start hauling it back to the building site.

Odina got up and started breakfast. The children were up doing their chores before breakfast. Yano checked on Sloppy and asked if he wanted breakfast. "It should be ready in fifteen minutes."

Sloppy said, "Yes, he would be there."

Alan told Odina he would ride down and check on the Coles after breakfast, then he needed to go see Clyde Bolin. He wanted to see if Clyde and his son, Lucas, would help with the building of the house. Alan showed Sloppy the plans he had drawn up for the house and asked him if he would supervise the beginning of the construction, since he would be out of town for three days.

Sloppy said, "shoot, we might have it finished by the time you get back, then laughed a little.

Alan laughed and said, "that would be great."

After breakfast, Yano was told to go saddle up the horses, so they could ride down and check on the Coles. "I want to show you and Sloppy the area where I want to build the house and the size of it. Y'all can start by gathering rocks for the foundation. There's plenty of rocks close by that will work."

When Alan, Yano and Sloppy rode up to the location where the Coles were camped, they were met with the biggest smiles on each of their faces. Alan knew he was doing the right thing and knew it would be better when he had a more suitable dwelling for them to live in. They could tell Eliza had been cooking over an open fire. They told them they slept the best last night that they had in a while.

Alan said, "I'm glad and we are glad to have you here. Henry, come walk with me, I want to show you where we are going to build the house. I see you have already found that spring. That is good water."

"Yessur, its sho is," said Henry. Misser Adams, I's could digs a well, ifin it's alright with you. I's dug lots of wells befo."

"Well Henry, if you think you can find water, you can do that, but I want you to help build this house first. You can get your water from that spring for the time being, then we could help you with the well. I want to get y'all a better shelter first."

"Yessur, I's does what you said. I's helps build, then digs a well. Days springs all under this ground, I's just knows it."

"Thank you, Henry, I have to go out of town for the next three days. Yano and Sloppy will start hauling lumber from the sawmill when it's available. While they are doing that, you and Tom can be gathering rocks to use for the foundation. There are plenty of good rocks to use close by. Come back up here and let me show you where to put stacks of them."

"Yessur."

Alan told Sloppy that he was going to see Clyde Bolin now and for him to stay there and supervise Yano, Henry and Tom tote rocks. "The floor would need to be one foot off the ground so have them put twelve or fifteen stacks in the general location of where we will need them, we'll square everything up when we start laying the big timbers down for the floor frame. Don't do anything Sloppy, just supervise okay?"

He just smiled and said, "Okay."

Riding down the path to the Bolins' house, he spotted Clyde working on a fence. "Howdy, old friend, how are you doing Clyde?"

"Doing well Alan, just fixing this broken fence. Come on, let's sit on the porch and have a cold drink of water."

"Sounds good," said Alan. "Clyde, I just stopped by to tell you that I have hired a family to help me with tending cattle, putting up more fencing and other chores that need to be done. In a few weeks, I will be through with the mining business, and I am going to raise cattle to sell."

"That sounds like a good plan Alan, but you don't have to tell me about hiring folks."

"I know I don't, but this is a Negro family, freed slaves, looking to make a better life for themselves."

"Shucks Alan, you know I don't care about that. I'm Swedish and Tehya is Shawnee, Negros are like us, just a little darker."

"I'm going to build a house on the south end of my property for them to stay in and wanted to know if you and Lucas could help us with that project?"

"Be glad to and I know Lucas will too, when he's not busy with being his brother's deputy. Ridge has two deputies now and only calls on them when needed, which ain't too often."

"Thank you, my friend, I got Sloppy to supervise, so he won't do any hard work, his health is not the best, but this gives him something to do. I won't be back until Wednesday night, but Yano and Sloppy will be hauling lumber from the sawmill as they can get it. I have the plans drawn up should they start before I get back."

Clyde said, "I will ride over there and check on them tomorrow to see what they have so far. I'll tell Lucas tonight when he gets home."

"Thanks Clyde, I really appreciate it."

Chapter 11

Standing at the train station in Rockford, Virginia, Alan was waiting to take his last train ride home. It was the end of August, and he had worked his last day at the Stockburn Coal Mining Company in Rockford, Virginia. He had said his goodbyes to all of his co-workers and again he spoke of his gratitude to Mr. Stockburn for hiring him so many years ago. He really loved the coal mining business and knew it well, but now it was time to live out his dream of surviving on his own land with his family.

Having gathered all of his belongings from his hotel room that had been his home for the last few years, three days a week, he sat in his seat on the train as it started to move. He was anxious to see what his house building crew had done since he had been gone. It was dark when Alan made it home and Odina had him a big bowl of potato soup with some corn fritters and coffee. He asked how everybody was. Odina said, "we are fine, Sloppy's fine, and the Coles are doing great, still smiling."

Alan finished up his supper and took a cup of coffee with him out to the porch to enjoy the night looking at the stars and listening to the sounds of the Appalachian Mountains.

Yano heard his father come in, so he got out of bed and went out on the porch to tell him what they had done on the house. When he was there helping and while he was sixty miles away working in Rockford, three days a week, they were able to get the house dried in and the tin roof on.

Alan told Yano how proud he was of all of them, and he was excited to go there tomorrow to see all they had done.

Yano said, "Sloppy had been enjoying being the boss, but he gets tired easily. We are not letting him work too much, mostly he just sits and points to what needs to be done. Tom is a hard worker like his dad and is my friend, but Father, Tom and Fanny can't read or write. I showed Tom how to write his name on the ground and that seemed to excite him. I think this is a good thing you've done for them Father; they are a nice family."

"I do too Yano and I think it's nice of you to do for them what you do. It's getting late, I'm tired and going to bed. We will talk more tomorrow."

"Good night, Father."

"Good night, Yano."

The next morning, Ayita, Koda and Nokomis were off to school.

Alan checked on Sloppy.

Sloppy said he would be there a little later today, he needed to go into town first.

Alan didn't question him, just said, "okay, we'll see you when you get there."

Alan and Yano arrived at the Cole's camp site and started to work on the chimney. Alan was amazed at how much they had done in the last three days. Lucas and Henry were finishing up the inside walls and Tom was stuffing hay behind the boards as they went up for insulation. The house had the same layout as Alan's house, except it was not a log cabin and it was a little bigger. It took a lot of lumber, but it was built well.

While in town, Sloppy went to a new store that sold wood stoves and wood and coal heaters. He purchased a wood stove for the kitchen and a wood or coal heater for additional heat in the front room. The winters got very cold, and these would keep the house warm.

They saw Sloppy riding up to the house in a wagon with two men following him. As they got closer, Alan could see a wood stove in the wagon and a wood heater, also. Alan smiled and told Yano that Sloppy had gone and bought them a brand-new wood stove and heater. "Sloppy is a very good man and very secretive when doing good deeds for people."

Yano said, "yes, he is."

Sloppy had the men pull the wagon around back, so they could unload the heavy stove right into the kitchen and the heater could be placed on the floor in the big room to be set up later.

Eliza saw the stove and with tears in her eyes said, "I can cook some fine meals on that stove." That made everybody smile.

Alan and Yano had finished the chimney, but the gray clay mortar they used would need to dry before they could build a fire in the fireplace. They finished installing the wood stove in the kitchen and it was ready for the cooking to begin. A lot of progress had been made on the house because of the hard work from so many friends working together. Everyone there worked hard and knew what they were doing.

Alan told Henry once the house was finished, they would start on a barn and a fence in a lot more areas.

Everybody was sitting on the porch of the new house in the shade, drinking some cool spring water while taking a break. They heard horses coming up the path to the house, it was Odina, Nokomis. Ayita and Koda. Odina had two cloth bags tied over her horse's back. Alan knew that she had brought food. Odina hopped off her horse and went to Eliza with the two bags of food supplies. Koda went to Yano and Tom and told them about his day at school. Tom had a yearning to learn things like his new friends were. Ayita and Nokomis went to Fanny, and they started running around in front of the house, playing and laughing. The grownups just sat there and smiled at the children's excitement as they played together. Sloppy was sitting on the edge of the porch enjoying a chew of tobacco and thinking if he was that young again, he could run all over these mountains for another forty years.

Then all of a sudden, they heard a scream, and Fanny came running back to the porch yelling, "a snake bit me!"

Everybody ran to Fanny to check her out for a snake bite. Sloppy ran as fast as a seventy-three-year-old man could to where Fanny came from. Then, they heard a shot. Sloppy came back up to the porch and said, "Diamondback Rattler, did it bite her?"

"Yes," Alan said, "she has a bite on her hand."

Sloppy said, "let me have her, cut me a strip of cloth for a tourniquet."

Eliza was upset and kept saying, "Lord, save my baby, Oh Lord, helps my baby."

Sloppy told Fanny to try and calm down and slow her breathing down. "You will be alright, but you have to be still and calm, Okay?"

Fanny responded with, "I's try Missur Sloppy, I's try."

Sloppy told Alan to hold her and turn her head away from what he was doing. He then took his knife and cut two small X's on the back of her hand where the snake had bitten her. He removed the wad of chewing tobacco from his mouth and set it on the porch and began to suck the poison out. As he spit out what he had sucked out of her little hand, he took that wad of chewing tobacco and packed it over the bite marks. Then, he took another strip of cloth and wrapped her hand, holding that tobacco in place. The tobacco should continue to draw the poison out. He loosened the tightness of the tourniquet and said they needed to get her to Dr. Clark in town.

It would take too long to hitch up the mules to the wagon, so Ayita said Fanny could ride on the back of her horse with her. Odina said that Eliza could ride on the back of hers. "Let's go, said Odina."

Alan told Odina to tell Dr. Clark that they would take care of everything, just take care of Fanny.

Sloppy walked over to his horse and pulled a bottle of whiskey out of his saddlebag. He wanted to rinse his mouth out because of having the venom of the snake in his mouth. He took a big swig and swished it around in his mouth, then spit it out. He felt a burning sensation in his cheek and remembered he had bitten the inside of his cheek the day before and the alcohol made it burn. He swallowed the next big swig of whiskey. A scene that was rarely ever seen, two Negro females riding on the back of bareback horses with two Indian females, galloping at a fast pace south on Three Bears Trail. When they reached Dr. Clark's office, they were met at the front by his nurse, Nova Bolin Morris. Nova was Clyde Boin's daughter who was now married to Larry Morris that owns the sawmill. Odina told her that Fanny was bitten by a Diamondback Rattlesnake. Dr. Clark stepped out from his office and said, "bring her back here." They helped Fanny get on the bed in the examining room. Dr. Clark said, "what is going on with this young lady?"

Odina said, "a rattlesnake bite on her hand. It was a Diamondback rattler. Her name is Fanny Cole, and this is her mother, Eliza Cole."

"Pleased to meet you both, now let's take a look at this bite." He first removed the tourniquet, then the wrapped hand. He asked Nova to wash her hand with warm soapy water. He asked if Odina could walk down to Mr. Dobbs store and get a large potato."

Ayita spoke up and volunteered to do that.

Dr. Clark said, "tell him to put it on my bill, I need it for a medical procedure."

Odina knew what he was going to use the potato for, but didn't know if Eliza knew or not. "The tobacco y'all put on this bite helped draw the poison out and so will a potato." Odina spoke up and said, "Sloppy did all of this. He cut those two X marks over the bite marks and sucked the poison out best he could."

Dr. Clark said, "he did real good and I'm sure young lady, you will be just fine. You'll need to stay here tonight and just lay still so I can keep an eye on you. We will know more after twenty-four hours, but I think you'll be well enough to go home tomorrow afternoon."

Eliza told Dr. Clark, "Doctor, I's got no money to pay you with but I could's do some cleaning or cooking for you iffin yous would lets me."

Dr. Clark said, "don't worry about that, let's just get her well."

Eliza said that she would stay with her if that was alright. "I's can jus sits in this here chair."

Ayita returned with two large potatoes and Dr. Clark made a potato poultice and applied it to the wound. He instructed Nova to change it every two hours. It should continue to draw out any remaining poison from her hand.

All but Eliza stepped out of the room. Odina told Dr. Clark, "We will pay the medical bill on Fanny, just let us know what we owe."

"Okay, Odina and tell Sloppy he saved her life by acting so fast. Her hand is not swollen as bad as it would have been had he not acted so fast. Her breathing is good, her throat and tongue are not swelling any and that's a good thing."

Ayita wanted to stay the night with her friend, but Odina said, "no, you come home with me, and we will come back tomorrow. Odina told Eliza that they would leave now, so they could tell the men folks what was going on. I know they are worried."

"Yessum, I's thanks you for what you does Ms. Odina."

Nova told Odina she would stay the night, also, so Dr. Clark could catch a nap or two.

"Thanks Nova, we will see you in the morning."

Odina and Ayita rode up to the house and told the men folks what the doctor said, you could see a big relief on their faces. She said, "he wanted her to stay the night so they could keep an eye on her. Eliza is staying with her, so she won't be scared. Dr. Clark said that you, Sloppy, saved her life by acting so fast and doing what you did." Odina told Henry that she would go back to town tomorrow to check on Fanny and if the Doctor released her, she would bring them home. "Yessum, I's sho does thanks you mam." Odina told Nokomis to come back home with her and Ayita. Alan said, "We will be home shortly, we have a few more things to get done here."

Alan and Odina both couldn't help but remember that just a few years ago they had almost lost their daughter to a crazy man that was as mean as a rattlesnake and understood how Henry and Eliza were feeling.

The next morning, Odina took the buckboard into town and let Ayita miss school and go with her. If Fanny was okay and released, she could give them a ride back home.

When they arrived at Dr. Clark's office, they were pleased to hear that she had a good night and would be ready to go in a couple of hours. The doctor wanted her to soak her hand in warm Epsom salt water two times, one hour apart, before he released her. He said she had no fever; no breathing problems and the swelling had already gone down on her hand. She should be good as new in a day or two and he would like to see her in a week for a checkup.

Odina left the Dr's office to visit Beanstalk at the Trading Post. She had some Indian jewelry to try and sell him. If he bought it, she would purchase some food supplies for her family and the Coles. Beanstalk was always happy to see Odina, her jewelry sold very well for him, so he purchased all that she had except two necklaces. With that money, Odina walked next door to Mr. Dobbs General Store and got her food supplies.

When she got back to the Dr's office, Fanny was sitting in the front room with her mother, Eliza, and her friend, Ayita. Dr. Clark said she could go home now, but he wanted her to soak her hand in a pan or bucket of warm Epsom salt water twice a day for a couple of days.

"Here's a bag of Epsom salt to use. Just put half a cup in the warm water."

Eliza thanked the Dr. and Nova for all they had done for her daughter.

Odina and Eliza were up front in the buckboard, the girls were riding in the back sitting on a pile of blankets that Odina had put in there to make their ride softer. Just as they were leaving, Koda and Nokomis had just got out of school and rode up to follow them to the Cole's house. On the ride home, Odina took out the two necklaces she kept out of her bag that she sold to Beanstalk and gave one to Eliza and Fanny as a friendship gift. They loved them and thanked her many times.

Back at the house, the men had been busy. They had built three rope beds, a table to eat from and finished installing the windows up in the gable. There were enough windows in the house to light it up during the day.

Sloppy didn't come out today, he said he was going to just rest in his shanty and sit on the porch drinking coffee. Alan thought he was afraid that Fanny would be sicker and that he didn't do enough. They would tell him when they got home that she was home and doing well.

Chapter 12

When Odina, Eliza, Fanny, Ayita, Koda and Nokomis arrived at the Cole's house, everyone was happy to see Fanny was doing better. They fixed her bed up for her to rest while Odina carried in the food supplies, she had purchased for them.

All of the Adams left the Coles to go home. Alan told Yano and Koda to put the horses up. Odina and the girls went in to start supper. Alan walked over to the shanty to check on Sloppy. His door was closed, so he knocked and called his name. He heard Sloppy's weak voice say, "yeah."

Alan walked in, Sloppy was lying in bed not looking good. Alan asked, "what's wrong Sloppy?"

Sloppy said, "I'm jest a little tired and don't feel good."

Alan said he would get Dr. Clark to come out.

Sloppy said, "No, just let me sleep. I'll be better in the morning. How's the girl?"

Alan said, "she is going to be alright. She came home today and looked really good, they said she had a good night. Doc said you did good and probably saved her life Sloppy."

"I'm glad, she's a tough little girl like Ayita is. I've seen grown men die from a snake bite like that."

Alan asked Sloppy if he could get him anything.

In a hard to hear response, Sloppy said, "No, I'll just sleep, that's what I need."

"Okay my friend, I'll check on you in the morning." Alan walked back to his house; he couldn't understand why Sloppy felt so bad. *Is it just tiredness or something else? Did he work too much? Is this another one of Sloppy's secrets, that only he knows the answer to? He had no air when speaking, just like when he had pneumonia a few years ago. He didn't show any signs of pneumonia yesterday when saving Fanny's life.* Alan told Odina that something was not right with Sloppy. "He said he was just tired, but I think it is more than that. He wouldn't let me go get Dr. Clark, said he would be better in the morning after a good night's sleep."

Worried about their friend, no sleep would come for Alan and Odina. Both were up before daylight. They had made a pot of coffee and Odina was making some

Ginseng tea. They knew he would drink both and it might just perk him up. Alan sat on his porch drinking his coffee and staring down at the shanty, wanting to go check on Sloppy, but wanting him to sleep longer if he could, so he waited.

When Odina said the Ginseng tea was ready, Alan took a small boiler of tea and a small boiler of coffee down to Sloppy. He could hear Sloppy moaning inside and knew that it was not good. Alan opened his door and went inside. Sloppy could not swallow, his throat had swollen, and his tongue appeared to be swollen.

Alan could hear his children out doing their chores. He called for Yano to come. He told Yano, "ride into town and get Dr. Clark to come out here fast, Sloppy is very sick and we don't know what's wrong with him. He's in a lot of pain and not breathing well."

Yano asked his father if Koda could go, "I would like to stay with Sloppy."

Understanding the bond that Yano had with Sloppy, he agreed to send Koda, but he wanted Ayita to go with him. Yano ran to tell Koda and Ayita to get their horses and ride into town and get Dr. Clark to come there fast, Sloppy was very sick and in a lot of pain.

Ayita and Koda took off riding bareback. When they got to the Dr's office, they were met inside by Nova. She asked what was wrong, both of you are out of breath. Koda told her that Sloppy was very sick and in a lot of pain. "We don't know what is wrong with him because he can barely talk. Father said for Dr. Clark to come quickly."

Nova said Dr. Clark rode out to check on Mr. Chandler early this morning, but should be back soon and she would tell him. Koda said, "Thank you, Nova, hope he can come soon."

When Ayita and Koda were leaving the Dr's office, they saw Dr. Lovie Hogue leaving the Tibbs Dinin' Hall. Dr. Hogue was in his eighties now and had retired, but would still come by once in a while and help Dr. Clark out some. Dr. Hogue started getting in his buggy and was approached by Ayita and Koda. He said, "Well, hello Ayita and Koda, what are you doing in town so early? Come here Ayita, let me look at your face. Well, well, well, that scar is completely gone now. We came to get

Dr. Clark, but he's gone to check on somebody. Sloppy is really sick and in a lot of pain. Father sent us to town to get the Dr. Could you come out there Dr. Hogue?"

Dr. Hogue asked, "What can you tell me about Sloppy?"

Koda said, "two days ago he was fine, but this young girl got bit by a rattlesnake on her hand and Sloppy sucked the poison out."

Dr. Hogue said, "sure, I'll ride out there, let me go by the Dr's office first and get some things. Tell your father, I'll be there shortly."

Yano was sitting next to Sloppy's bed, hoping the Dr. could fix him up again. Sloppy pulled Yano down to his face to talk to him. He told him to remember the place he told him to look for something out of place. Yano said, "I remember."

Then Sloppy told him, "when good people need help, help them if you can. Stay away from bad people. Keep some secrets in order to keep you and your family safe. You will soon know my secrets, share my secrets with your father. Share my treasures with your family and always try to help good people when they are down on their luck. Remember me telling you where I wanted to be buried?"

"Yes, I remember Sloppy, but hope it's years away."

"It's okay Yano, I have lived the most wonderful life for the past forty years in those mountains. I have many treasures hidden there, but my favorite treasure is you and your family. Now, get your father to come back in please. Okay."

Ayita and Koda came riding up telling their father that Dr. Hogue was coming.

"Dr. Hogue?"

"Yes, Dr. Clark was out on a call, and we saw Dr. Hogue coming out of Tibbs Dining Hall, so we asked him, he said he would be here shortly."

"Y'all did good and I am proud of you both." Alan went in and asked Sloppy if there was anything he could do for him. He motioned for Alan to come closer. Sloppy said he sure would like to see Fanny, so he would know she was alright.

Alan said, "We will get her here."

Odina told Yano and Koda to hitch her horse to the buckboard quickly. Ayita said she would go too but would ride Nokomis's horse, hers had been ridden hard for six miles. Odina and Ayita arrived at the Cole's place in a few minutes and asked if Fanny could come to see Sloppy if she felt like it. He's really sick and wanted to see her to make sure she was alright. All of you can come too, that's why I brought the buckboard."

Eliza said, "She's jus fine now thanks to Mr. Sloppy."

Henry spoke up and said he would hitch up the mules and he and Tom would come along behind them, so they would have a ride back. Fanny hopped on the back of the horse that Ayita was riding, and Eliza got in the buckboard with Odina. When they got to Three Bears Trail, they could see Dr. Hogue ahead of them.

Dr. Hogue arrived before Odina. He went in to see Sloppy to try to find out what brought on this sick spell he was having. Dr. Hogue already knew what it was, and it was not good. During his examination of Sloppy, he noticed his tongue was badly swollen and dark purple in color. He also noticed a cut on his inner cheek and the skin color was very dark. Sloppy told Dr. Hogue that his jaw was painful. Dr. Hogue said, "I can give you something for the pain, and it will make you sleepy, so you can rest, but, before I do, did you have a cut in your mouth when you sucked that poison out of that little girls hand?"

Sloppy said, "Yes, but I didn't remember it until I rinsed my mouth out with whiskey, and it burned."

Dr. Hogue took a bottle of liquid morphine from his black bag and drew a certain amount into a syringe, then squirted it in Sloppy's mouth. Dr. Hogue stepped out of the shanty to see all of the Adams and a Negro family standing around the porch of the shanty.

Alan said that Sloppy requested to see this little girl, Fanny, that got bit by the rattlesnake.

Dr. Hogue said, "You better hurry, I gave him something for pain and he will be asleep shortly."

Alan took Fanny by the hand and led her to Sloppy's bedside as Eliza followed. Standing there with a scared look on her face, Sloppy opened his eyes and motioned for her to come closer. He gently took her hand and tried to look at it, then smiled.

Fanny smiled back and said, "Thanks you Misser Sloppy for what you does for me."

Sloppy closed his eyes, Alan then led Fanny and Eliza back outside.

Dr. Hogue motioned for Alan to come over to the side of the shanty. He told Alan that Sloppy had a cut on his inner cheek when he sucked the venom out and even though he spit it out, some of the poison got into his system. He said he didn't remember the cut in his mouth until he rinsed his mouth out with whiskey, and it burned. It was too late, the poison got in his system instantly and there would have been nothing they could have done then and there is nothing we can do now except make him comfortable. His throat is swollen, and it is a dark purple color. The poison has already spread to his brain and organs. His body will shut down within the next hour. "I'm sorry, I know Sloppy is a good friend and he did a good thing by saving that little girl's life. That shows Sloppy's good character. He knew he had to try and help her."

"Yes, I know Doc, he was worried that he didn't do enough, that's why he wanted to see her. He knows he is dying and is okay with the life he had lived, but I sure hate to see him go."

Alan gathered his family to stand by Sloppy's bedside. One by one, they told him they loved him. Alan told him, "Thank you for your friendship Sloppy, you have been our greatest treasure."

Sloppy took his last breath with a smile on his face. Dr. Hogue looked at Alan and just shook his head as he pulled the blanket over Sloppy's head. When they stepped out of the shanty, they could see all four of the Cole family, they had their heads bowed and you could see tears running down Fanny's face.

There was a Red Tail Hawk circling over the shanty. Odina said that the Red Tail Hawk was Sloppy's spirit bird. Always protect it.

Dr. Hogue said he would write up the death certificate. Alan said, "I will bring his body to town for the undertaker to prep him for burial and I will get Delmar Betts to build a nice casket for him, we will take care of the burial and honor his wishes."

Chapter 13

It had been five days since Sloppy passed away and now Alan and Yano were over halfway to having him at his final resting place. They had a nice service at the Primitive Baptist Church. Delmar Betts built a casket for Sloppy to be buried in. In attendance at the funeral were, Alan Adams family, most of Clyde Bolin's family, Henry Cole's family, Dr. Hogue, Dr. Clark, Beanstalk from the Trading Post, Rooster from the Tavern, The Morris brothers from the sawmill and many other towns people. Preacher John Woods preached the service and Alan spoke a few words, telling what a good friend Sloppy was to him and his family. He was a true mountain man that loved surviving in the mountains for over forty years. The mountains were where he felt the most peace and the mountains would be his final resting place per his request.

With his casket loaded on the wagon, being pulled by Sloppy's mule, they brought along the tools they would need and enough food supplies for a few days. Delmar

Betts made a marker for his grave that read --*Willard "Sloppy" Floyd ---1792---1865 A True Mountain Man.*

As they were riding, Yano said to his father, "Sloppy had secrets, more secrets than anyone knew. A few years ago, he told me how to find his secrets, but not to search for them until he died and don't tell anyone except you and mother after he died."

Alan looked at his son and said, "I knew Sloppy had secrets that nobody knew including me, just like we have secrets that we didn't share."

"Sloppy told me where to look after he died, but to have you with me when I looked, not to search alone."

"Well, Yano, that's good advice."

It was slow going pulling the wagon up the narrow path to Sloppy's cabin, but they made it.

Yano told his father that Sloppy had changed his mind about where he wanted to be buried. "He told me to remember and carry out his wishes and that he wanted his final resting place to be beside his cabin instead of the chair tree location." Yano hopped off the wagon and walked up a small hill to the right of the cabin where there is a flat piece of land and said, "This is the spot he told me he wished to be buried at."

"Okay, that's where it will be."

After digging the grave, they had to use the mule to drag the casket to the grave. When the casket was covered with dirt, they started gathering rocks to place on top. They put his marker at the head of the grave and then sat on the ground next to it. Tired, but happy they were able to fulfil Sloppy's wishes.

They heard the call of a Hawk and looked up to the sky and saw a Red Tail Hawk circling directly over their head. Yano said, "I think Sloppy's spirit is pleased."

"Me too Son."

It was still early with plenty of light left and Yano wanted to search for Sloppy's secret place while they were there.

Alan said, "Okay, where do we start?"

"About a half of a mile down the path to the chair tree, but we have to get lined up with a stack of rocks, the chair tree and the rock cliff. We will have to take a lot of rope and probably the short handle shovel. He also told me to be careful and watch out for a mountain lion that frequents that mountain where the rock cliffs are."

They unloaded their food supplies and put them in the cabin and put Sloppy's mule in the corral with food and water. Then they started walking down to the chair tree carrying two long ropes and a short handle shovel. Reaching the chair tree, they waded across the creek and climbed to the top of a small hill and found the stack of rocks. Yano told his father that this was the place that Sloppy wanted him to retrieve the rope from a few years ago that he said was hanging down from the top of the rock cliff. "We have to line up in a straight line with the chair tree and the stack of rocks at the top of the rock cliff.: Yano picked out an oak tree at the top of the rock cliff that lined up perfectly."

Alan let his son do all the finding of this secret location.

Yano explained to his father that they would need to climb that mountain and go to that oak tree to stay in line with the chair tree and stack of rocks. From there, they would repel down about twenty feet to a ledge, then look for something out of place.

Chapter 14

Alan smiled and said, "Sounds like ole Sloppy was a little secretive in giving you these instructions. Probably because he knew what a good tracker you are. He really took a liking to you from an early age. He could see you carried the Spirit of the Wolf in you."

"Let's get going, we can go to our right before we start our climb. It's not as steep and will make climbing up to the top easier." Yano went to the oak tree he spotted from below and said, "this is the oak tree that lines up with the chair tree and stacks of rocks." They took their rope and wrapped one end around the oak tree, then tied both ends together and threw the knotted end over the cliff. They would use the rope to repel down to a ledge.

Yano went first and when he landed on the ledge, he told his father that he saw mountain lion tracks on the ledge. Bringing the shovel with him, Alan repelled down to the ledge. He could also see the mountain lion tracks. The place looked very similar to Sloppy's best friend, Fred Smith's hiding place. Thinking they must have spoken of a perfect hiding place where strangers would not just walk by. The ledge was big enough for Yano and Alan to stand on.

As Yano stared at the location, looking for something out of place, he spotted different colored flat rocks on the floor of the ledge. Looking under a low hanging rock shelf, he saw what looked like an X mark, made with the different colors of rocks. He had to study it for a few minutes before he could see the X mark, but to him, it looked out of place. Yano now knew that this was the spot and so did Alan, as he watched his son discover it.

Yano looked at his father and said, "This is the spot, I just know it is."

Alan said, "I think you are right Yano." Alan instructed Yano to remove the rocks before he started digging at the spot, so he could put them back just like they were.

"Yes sir," then he started digging and hit something that sounded like wood instead of rock.

Alan sat on the ledge watching his son and knew that he had found Sloppy's treasure.

Yano said, "It's a wood box buried here," as he kept digging. He dug all around the box, but he could not lift it out of the hole. The box was larger than the one Alan found.

Alan tried to help Yano lift the box from the hole, but he couldn't. Alan told Yano to pry the lid off. When he removed the lid, he found a leather pouch on top of a lot of cloth bags that were full of something. He opened the leather pouch first and found several papers inside with writing on them. As he read the first paper, Sloppy was saying that, at the time of his death, he left these eight hundred acres of land, the log cabin and all of its contents to Yano Adams, the first born to Alan and Odina Adams. Signed----*Willard 'Sloppy' Floyd.* There were several more papers to look at, some were maps of the land and others had what appeared to be writings from Sloppy to Yano. He would read them later back at the cabin.

They started removing the cloth bags and looked inside them. They were all full of gold and Alan was guessing that there was fifty or sixty pounds of gold in the box. Both were sitting on the ground on the ledge, just amazed at the amount of gold that Sloppy had hidden. They understood now more than ever why Sloppy enjoyed the hunt more than the value of what he had found. They will miss their friend and would rather have him still here than all of the gold, but he's gone now, and his wish was to leave all of his worldly goods to Yano.

Alan asked Yano what he wanted to do about all of this?

Yano said that he would like to take one bag of gold with them and all of the paper notes, then put all of the other bags back in the box and cover it back like it was. So, Yano fixed the place back like it was.

Alan had always been proud of Yano and all of his children, but at this moment, he knew that Yano understood the meaning of friends over treasures of gold. Both were good, but a good friend is more valuable.

When they repelled down to the bottom, they untied the knot at the end of the rope and pulled it down. They left no sign that they were ever there.

When they got back to the cabin, they started cooking up a supper of fried potatoes with chunks of ham. Alan made him a pot of coffee.

After supper, Yano took the coal oil lamp and sat it on the table, so he could read the rest of the papers Sloppy had put in the leather pouch. Alan took a cup of coffee and sat on the porch. Looking over his left shoulder, he could see Sloppy's marker at his grave up on the rise beside the cabin. Yano came out on the porch after reading all of Sloppy's notes. He would read them over and over when he got home, where he had better light.

"Did Sloppy leave any advice for you to follow in his notes Yano?"

"Yes, he did Father, he told me to share with family, respect people, wildlife and the land. Help good people when they are down on their luck if I could. Stay away from bad people. He, also, wrote for us to check the shanty real good for something hidden there. He wrote for me to be cautious around an old female mountain lion that he named Isabell, she could be aggressive and a large bear, he called Grumpy because he was usually angry."

Just at that moment, they heard the eerie scream of a mountain lion that sounded like it was on top of the mountain where they were earlier.

Yano said, "It's probably Isabell, the aggressive female that Sloppy wrote about."

They planned to head back home early in the morning, so they turned in for the night. Tired, but feeling good about what they accomplished. They fell asleep pretty quick.

Chapter 15

Alan and Yano were riding together in the wagon, going home and enjoying their time talking with each other. Mostly about Sloppy and how good he was to people in his sneaky way. "Like when he bought you those two guns or when he bought the horse for Nokomis or the gifts he gave to Ayita and Koda. Did you know that Sloppy paid for the lumber from the sawmill that built the house for the Coles to live in?"

Yano said he did not know, but he knew that Sloppy bought the wood stove and wood heater for them.

Alan told Yano they had more to do to help the Coles get better situated and Sloppy enjoyed being a big part of it, in his secret sneaky kind of way.

"Now that I'm no longer working at the coal mines, we will plan a trip down to High Point, West Virginia, to see my mother and father. They have never met Ayita, Koda or Nokomis and you were very young the only time you met them. We will go to the village your mother is from and visit with her people. Her mother and father died years ago, but some of her relatives and friends may still be there. Y'all will learn more about your heritage. When we go, we will have Henry to look after our place and livestock. We will put a cover on the wagon and load it down with the supplies that we will need on our travels. It takes about two days to get there and two days to get back, and we will probably stay a couple of days."

It was afternoon the next day when Alan and Yano pulled up to the porch of their house. Odina, Ayita, Koda and Nokomis came out to greet them back home.

Odina said, "We are glad you and Yano are home."

"We are too," said Alan" Alan handed the bag of food supplies that was left to Ayita and Nokomis and told them to put it up in the kitchen. Koda helped Yano put the mule and wagon up at the barn. Alan said, "Give Sloppy's mule some extra oats."

Alan took the heavy bag of gold inside and asked Odina if she thought it would fit in their hiding place, he was pretty sure the bag of gold weighed over five pounds.

Odina replied, "that's a lot of gold, is it some that Sloppy left?"

"Yes, and I will tell you all about our trip later, but right now I sure would like to have a cup of coffee and just sit on the porch for a while."

Odina joined Alan on the porch as he was drinking a cup of coffee. He asked her how the Coles were doing. She said, "they are doing fine, Henry and his family have come here every day to check on us. I offered to teach Fanny and Tom how to read and write if they would like to. They smiled as they nodded their heads yes. Henry said that would be nice and they would have a better chance at a better life if they could read and write."

Alan started telling Odina about their trip. "After we laid Sloppy to rest at his requested spot, I learned that he had given Yano instructions a few years ago on how to find his treasures. Once I tell you of what we found, you will understand why sloppy preferred mountain life and having good friends over all of his treasures. He loved the hunt for treasures and to be able to use it to help good people in need. He left a few notes to Yano. One of the notes said that he leaves his eight hundred acres and cabin to Yano. All of the treasures should be shared with family and when he could, help someone having a hard time. We certainly didn't take the time to locate all that he had hidden, but what we did find shows that he had been hiding treasures for over forty years. He kept his secrets well."

Odina said, "we sure miss Sloppy, especially Yano, they had such a tremendous bond."

Alan told Odina that he wanted to take all of their family to see his parents and her kinfolks and friends in the village. "Our children need to know more about their heritage and meet family."

Odina said, "that would be good, it's been a long time."

Chapter 16

While Alan and Yano were gone to Sloppy's place to lay him to rest, Henry Cole was busy building things at the place they call home. He built an outhouse, counters in the kitchen to prep food on, a table for them to have their meals at and had started digging a well. When Alan went over there, he was very impressed with what Henry had done. Henry was a very good carpenter. Alan showed Henry where he wanted to build a barn and where they would start putting up more pasture fencing. He had drawn up the plans for the barn with the measurements and a lumber list in order to get started.

One of the Morris brothers would deliver a wagon load of lumber every other day, once Alan gave them a list of what he wanted. With them making deliveries, it gave them more time to build the barn. In the next few days, they were able to frame up the barn and start on the rafters. With Yano and Tom helping, the barn was going up pretty fast. In the afternoon, when they stopped for the day, Henry went back to digging the well.

It's been a couple of weeks now and the barn was finished. Henry had water in the well he dug, and Alan was thinking now would be a good time to make that trip with his family to High Point, West Virginia to see his mother and father and to visit the village Odina came from. Alan asked Henry if he could look after their place while they were gone and take care of his livestock. He told him he could get milk from the cow and eggs from the chickens. "Yessur, I's can do's that fer ya."

Three days later, Alan and his family were heading south to High Point. Alan and Odina were riding in the wagon, all of the children were riding their own horses. The wagon was loaded with their food, feed for the horses and mules, a barrel of water tied to the side of the wagon and two canvas tarps to be used to make tents for the children to sleep in. Alan also hid two bags of gold in the wagon, each bag weighing about two pounds. He wanted to help his parents if they needed it. They set up camp the first night at a creek that ran next to the path. Yano and Koda unhitched the mules, removed the saddles from the horses, let them drink water from the creek and would feed them some oats later. Ayita and

Nokomis volunteered to cook up some supper. Yano had built a fire for them to cook over and they fried up some potatoes and ham as Alan and Odina just sat on the ground admiring all of their children. The weather was good, and they all got a good night's sleep.

They were loaded up and on their way after breakfast, they should arrive at his parents' home after lunch.

When they got to his father's land, the first thing they saw was the little log cabin that they first lived in when they got married in 1847. That was where they lived until 1848. Now the little log cabin appeared to have a family of Negros living there. Alan could see some farming around the cabin and assumed that his father was sharecropping with that family. Another half a mile and they reached his parents' place.

He spotted his father and mother working in a garden beside their house. His parents had a confused look on their face as they rode up. Then, excited when they recognized their son. They walked toward the covered wagon that had their son and daughter-in-law in it and saw four younger people on horseback. Alan hopped off the wagon and hugged his mother and shook his father's hand. "It's been a long-time Father."

"Yes, it has Son. Good to see you."

Odina got down from the wagon and hugged both his parents.

Alan introduced their children, "this is Yano that you met about thirteen years ago, these are our twins, Ayita and Koda and our baby girl, Nokomis." All the children hugged their grandparents. Alan asked if they could put them up for a few days.

His father said, "we could put y'all up for a few years. We have missed all of you so much and wondered how everybody was doing."

"We have been doing very well, Father, but tell me how you and Mother have been? I saw a family of Negros, looked like they were living in the cabin that Odina and I lived in."

"Yeah, that's Willie Jones' family. He helps me here and we share-crop a little farming. I pay him a little when I can, and we share when we butcher beef and hogs. It doesn't take much for me and your mother, but Willie had four children and a wife to feed. They have been here about two years, and I needed a little help with chores, so it works great for both of us. They were slaves until 1863, they set out to make a better life when they were freed."

Alan said, "We have hired a family of Negros to help on our place. They are the Coles, and their story is just like the Jones story. The Coles are good people and hard workers. They are looking after our place and taking care of the livestock while we are here. How is the prospecting for gold down here now?"

His father said, "I still find a little off and on, but no large amounts. How is it where you are at Alan?"

Alan said, "excuse me a minute." He went to the wagon and retrieved two cloth bags and brought them in. He set the two cloth bags on the table in front of his father and said, it's pretty good up there off and on."

"My, my, my, that must be four pounds together, you have done well Alan. I knew you would."

"It is at least that, maybe more and I am giving this to you and Mother as a gift."

"No Son, we can't take that, you will need it to feed all of them children. We will make it alright; it doesn't take much for us."

Alan said, "we brought it for you and Mother, now quit fussing about it and put it in a hiding place. Father, we have two thousand acres of land with a nice log cabin that we live in and all of it is paid for by gold from this land. I worked the coal mines for over seventeen years. I got promotions and raises because of what you taught me as a young boy. We have had some sadness and sorrow, but much more joy and happiness. I have the most wonderful family and am so proud of all of them. My first best friend was Willard 'Sloppy' Floyd. We met Sloppy in 1848, the day after we bought our land and cabin. Sloppy was a true mountain man. A couple weeks ago, Sloppy died and me and Yano took him to his place in the Appalachian Mountains and buried him close to his cabin where he requested."

Alan asked his father if he could help him in the garden to finish up what he and his mother were doing when they rode up.

He said, "No, we can finish hoeing that garden tomorrow, we have a lot of catching up to do tonight."

Alan told Yano and Koda to put the horses and mules in the corral and make sure they had feed and water. Odina, Ayita and Nokomis went in the kitchen and talked with Awinita, Alan's mother. She was all smiles seeing her granddaughters and enjoying getting to know them.

Alan told his father about losing two miners in a cave in seventeen years ago. "I was made Safety Officer right after that because I determined that the cave in was caused by sandstone." He also told his father that five years ago, when Ayita was just seven, she was taken by a crazy Indian named Tunga. "We tracked him for three days before we caught up with him. He had a bad scar under his eye down to his lip. He burned a scar on Ayita's face just like his. We got Ayita home and won't have to worry about him hurting any other young girls again. Sloppy is the one that knew he was the one that took her. Sloppy and Yano were the first to start tracking them."

"Sounds like a very scary ordeal for Ayta, how is she now?"

"She's perfect, it made her a very strong little girl." They talked until late in the night, then Alan and Odina took the one extra bedroom, and the children laid out their bedrolls on the floor in the front room. The next morning after breakfast, Alan, Odina, Yano, Ayita, Koda and Nokomis all rode a few miles south to the village where Odina was raised. Her father and mother passed away years ago, but she wanted to see if any of her friends were still there or any of the elders that would remember her.

Chapter 17

Odina didn't see any of her friends as she rode through the village. She spotted an elderly woman sitting on the porch of an old log cabin at the end of the village and recognized her as Omawi. She told her family that she must talk to her as she rode up to her. Odina started speaking in Cherokee. Odina asked if she remembered her from being raised in this village years ago.

The elderly woman looked at Odina, smiled and said, "yes, she remembered her and her mother and father." Omawi had to be in her mid-nineties, the lines on her face told the story of a difficult past.

Alan and the children were gathered around her, listening to her speak. There were Indian children running around and playing. Yano spotted a beautiful Indian girl about his age walking by them. He smiled at her, and she smiled back. Yano then asked to be excused, so he could go talk with the most beautiful girl he had ever seen. He was not sure what he would say to her, but he had to say something.

When he caught up to her, he asked if she lived in this village.

She answered, "Yes, all of my life, where are you from?"

He said, "fifty miles north of here in Shepherd Springs. My mother is from this village. "

"What's your mother's name?" she asked?

"My mother is Odina Elu Adams, and my father is Alan Atohi Adams, he was raised just up the road in High Point."

She said, "I know Awinita Adams that lives just up the road, is she your grandmother?"

"Yes, she is, she is of the wolf clan in her tribe as is my mother."

"I am too," she said, "what is your name?"

"My name is Yano Phoenix Adams, I go by Yano. What's your name if I may ask?"

"You may, my name is like your mother's, my name is Elu-Ama."

Yano looked at her and said, "Beautiful Water, your name means Beautiful Water."

'That's what I have been told. That may be why I love the water so much. I am walking to a creek that flows into the Potomac River now to catch a few fish to eat."

Yano asked her if she would like to ride on the back of his horse to the creek instead of walking.

She said, "No, she wanted to walk, so she could explore things on the ground better, I have a fine horse that I usually ride, but today I prefer to walk."

"I understand," said Yano, "would you mind if I came with you? I love to explore and fish too?"

"Sure, I guess it will be alright. I enjoy talking with you."

Yano thought he was already in love. Whatever it was, it brought joy to his heart and helped to calm the sadness of losing his friend Sloppy. "Let me go tell my mother and father and I'll catch up with you."

Yano's father, mother, brother and sisters were still talking with Omawi and he should be there listening, but he had met someone that took his attention away from anything else, but talking with her. He told his parents that he wanted to go down to a creek with his new friend.

His father knew that this girl would get his mind off Sloppy, so he said, "go ahead, but don't stay too long, we need to spend more time with my parents."

Yano said he wouldn't be long and rode to catch up with Elu-Ama. When he got to her, he got off his horse and walked with her. As they walked toward the river, he watched her as she grabbed a grasshopper and put it in a little cloth pouch. She turned and said to Yano, "trout love grasshoppers." They continued walking, she told Yano to tie his horse up to a sapling away from the Mountain Laurel thicket. "The creek I want to fish in is just on the other side and it's too difficult for your horse to go."

Yano tied Smokie to a small sapling away from the Mountain Laurel. Mountain Laurel was toxic, and he didn't want Smokie grazing on the leaves.

Elu-Ama led Yano to the creek and said, "this is my favorite spot to fish or to just get in the water and cool off. Nobody ever comes to this spot. Most people will go down to the Potomac River where this creek runs into it to fish, they think this creek is too small."

Yano looked up and down the stream and could see many small waterfalls. There were large deep looking pools of water at the bottom of each small waterfall. Elu-Ama climbed up on a big boulder with a flat top and said, 'I fish here and sometimes swim in this deep hole of water." She removed a stick about four inches long from her pocket that had a fishing line, and a hook tied to it. She baited her hook with the grasshopper and threw it over in the pool of water. Just as soon as that grasshopper hit the water, she hooked a nice size trout. She asked Yano if he could find her something to use for bait and then said she could see three more trout down in the crystal-clear water and needed one more good one. She only took what she needed.

Yano went downstream from her, turned over a rock and caught a small spring lizard and brought it to her. He said, "trout loves spring lizards."

She smiled at him and said, "yeah, I know, thank you". They both laughed a little.

Yano was really smitten with this beautiful new friend. They were so much alike and appeared to share the same knowledge about many things. Elu-Ama caught another trout and said, "that's enough." She put the fish on a stringer and put them in the water until she was ready to go. She was not in a hurry because she was enjoying the company of Yano. They both laid back on the flat rock to feel the warmth of the sun and hear the water running over the rocks.

Yano told her that they would leave in a couple of days to go back home. He said, "we just came down here to check on my grandparent and to tell you the truth, I was ready to go back after we saw they were doing well, but now, I'm in no hurry."

Elu-Ama was in no hurry for Yano to leave either, but she would not speak about it because she knew he would be gone in a few days, and she would probably not ever see him again.

"How old are you, Elu-Ama?"

I am sixteen and you can call me Elu, everybody just calls me Elu."

"How old are you Yano?"

"I'm sixteen also," said Yano. "Bad as I hate to leave, I guess I need to be heading back to my grandparents' house to help with any chores they need me for. Would you like a ride back to the village?"

Elu had planned on staying longer at this location, but she really liked Yano and might never see him again. She said, "Yes, if you don't mind, I would appreciate a ride back."

Yano was all smiles as he gave Elu a hand up on Smokie's back. He was happy to spend a few more minutes with this beautiful girl. She had long black hair, an olive complexion and the sweetest dark brown eyes he had ever seen. He walked Smokie, so he would have more time with Elu.

When they got to the edge of the village, Elu said, "This is good and hopped off. Thanks for the ride, Yano, I am glad we met."

"Me too Elu and I hope to see you again sometime."

Yano arrived back at his grandparents' house to find his grandfather, his father and his brother Koda hoeing the garden. Yano grabbed a hoe and jumped in to help finish the last two rows. Alan could tell that Yano enjoyed meeting the beautiful girl because he had not stopped smiling.

Sitting at the supper table, Yano talked about his day with the beautiful girl named Elu-Ama. Looking at his mother, he said, "Yes, Mother, her name is Elu like yours."

Odina smiled at Yano; she enjoyed seeing the joy on her son's face especially after the sadness of Sloppy's death. After supper, all the men went to the porch to talk while the women were working in the kitchen and talking.

Alan told his father they would stay tomorrow and help him with anything he needed and would head back home the next day. He said they would come back to visit in a few months and would not wait for years to come next time. Yano heard that and just knew he needed to see Elu tomorrow one more time before they left. He was already planning to make the trip again sooner than that by himself.

Chapter 18

The morning before they were to leave to return home, Yano asked his father if he could go and try to find Elu to see her before they left the next day.

Alan could see how much Elu was helping Yano remove his sadness over losing Sloppy so he said, "Yes, Yano, go find your girl, we will take care of the chores here for my father."

Yano ate a little breakfast very quickly and asked to be excused.

Alan smiled at Yano and said, "go ahead and don't forget, we leave in the morning early."

"Yes sir", then he ran to the corral to get Smokie. He didn't bother with the saddle, just the bridle and he was off riding to the village. Riding through the village, he did not see Elu. Getting to the end of the village and not seeing Elu, the fear hit him that he may not find her. Then he saw the elderly Indian woman, Omawi sitting on her porch just like yesterday. When he rode up to her, he remembered she only spoke Cherokee, so in the Cherokee language, he said, "Omawi, do you remember me from yesterday? I'm Yano, my mother, father, brother and sisters talked with you yesterday."

In her frail voice Omawi said, "Yes, I remember you Yano, you carry the Spirit of the Wolf in your soul, you have seen and touched the Spirt Wolf. You left early yesterday and chase another spirit of a different kind."

Yano just looked at her with a puzzled look on his face.

Then she said, "You hold many secrets from a lost friend. The spirit you chased yesterday had gone to their favorite place to soak in the cool water and meditate."

Yano was amazed at how much Omawi knew about him, but he was in a hurry to find Elu, so he told Omawi "thank you," and headed to the spot where they were yesterday. When he got to the spot, there was a paint horse without a saddle tied to the same sapling that he tied Smokie to yesterday. He just knew this was her paint horse. He made his way through the Mountain Laurel and from a distance, he could see Elu laying on the flat rock. She was completely nude, soaking up the warmth of the sun with her clothes laid out beside her. He didn't want to alarm her, but he couldn't stop admiring her beauty. He thought she was soaking in the cool water and now just letting the sun warm her. Not only was she beautiful, but she looked so peaceful.

Yano backed his way back through the Mountain Laurel as quietly as he could. When he got back to where the horses were tied, he called her name. He heard her say, "Yano, I'm over here."

He said okay, I'm on my way." He walked slowly to give her time to get dressed. When he reached the rock, he saw her standing on the top fully dressed and smiling as though she was happy to see him. He climbed up to the top of the rock and stepped toward her and said, "I have missed you Elu." They embraced with a hug, and she said, "I have missed you too, Yano." Her hair was still wet, and her silky-smooth skin was glowing in the sunlight. They released their hug and looked into each other's eyes. Without saying another word, they kissed.

After the kiss, Elu said, "I don't want you to go, I've never met anyone like you."

Yano said, "I don't want to go either, but I have to. I could spend every minute with you, and I am already planning a return trip soon. My heart almost stopped beating when you first smiled at me. I thought of you all night. My father said we are leaving early in the morning to return home. It takes about two days to travel the distance between here and there. I knew I had to find you today, so I could tell you how I feel about you and we could learn more about each other. I want to tell you about my family and learn more about yours."

She said, "Well that woman you and your family were talking to yesterday is my great grandmother, Omawi. She is a spirit reader and she's one hundred years old. My father works in the coal mines over in High Point, my mother sews, cooks, gardens and makes jewelry to sell. I have two older brothers and one younger sister. All of us have been taught the Cherokee ways and heritage. We attended the white schools to learn how to read and write in English. I teach the younger children in our village English, reading and writing. This is a financially poor village, but rich with family and friends. Granny Omawi read your spirit yesterday just by looking into your eyes. She told me that you carried the Spirit of the Wolf in your soul too."

Yano interrupted her and asked, "she said I carry the spirit too? Who else did she say?"

Elu said, "Me, I carry the Spirit of the Wolf in my soul. I have heard them, seen them and touched them, but I can never find any sign that they were here."

Yano knew from the first time seeing and meeting her that this was meant to be. Now he was certain of it.

Yano said his father worked in the coal mines here in High Point years ago for eighteen years in Shepherd Springs and Rockford. "He has just retired and wants to live and survive on our land, hunting, fishing, trapping and raising cattle to sell. My mother cooks, sews, and makes jewelry to sell like your mother. My brother and sister under me are twins, then the youngest is our baby sister. We just buried a very dear friend of the family about two weeks ago. He lived with us for long periods of time in his elder years. We called him Sloppy, he taught me a lot about living and surviving in the mountains. Five years ago, my sister Ayita was taken by a crazy man. Me and Sloppy were the first to start tracking them. It took three days to catch up with him. My father found them and brought Ayita back home and made it so the crazy man would never harm another child. It's a long story and I'll tell you all about it one day but right now I want to spend the day with you."

"Elu, when is your birthdate?" Yano asked?

"My birthday is February 2, 1849, when is yours Yano?"

Yano's eyes got really big, and he said, t"his is another sign that we are meant to be together, my birthdate is February 2, 1849, also."

"Are you kidding me?" Elu asked?

"No, I swear, our birthdates are exactly the same." Yano said, "I know we have just met, but I feel like I have known you my whole life, and would like to know if I come back in about a month if I can see you again? I mean, if you're not planning on moving somewhere else, then I would come there, no matter the distance."

"No, I have no plans on going anywhere, and yes, you can see me. Most Indian girls spend their life with our tribe in this village unless, well, never mind."

"Unless what? Tell me.'"

"There have been many girls that married and moved off with their new husbands and many have married and stayed in the village with their husbands."

Yano said, "It sounds like our families are very similar. My mother was raised in this village. She, also, taught the children to read and write. When she married my father, they lived on my grandparents' land in a little log cabin. After a year, with dreams of owning their own land and raising a family, they took the chance and loaded up their belongings and traveled fifty miles to Shepherd Springs, Virginia then, now it's called West Virginia."

Elu said, "This day is passing too fast, and I don't want it to end."

Yano said, "It will be hard leaving in the morning for me, and you are to blame for that Elu. May I kiss you again, Elu?"

She lowered her head, lifted her eyes up to meet his and said, "Yes."

They kissed again, then held each other for a few minutes. The sun was already starting to set and they couldn't believe how fast the day had passed. Yano said, "I guess I need to get going, but I don't want to."

Elu said, "I need to go also, but I don't want to."

They started walking back to their horses, and when they got to them, they kissed again. They both hopped on their horses and Elu started to ride off toward the village.

Yano yelled to her to hold up. He rode up beside her, leaned over to her and kissed her again. He then told her, "one month, I'll be back in one month."

She said, "I'll be waiting for you, Yano Adams."

Chapter 19

The Adams had been home now for a week. Alan and Yano had helped Henry finish the barn. Henry and his son, Tom, had done a lot of work while Alan and his family were gone. They completed digging the well, Henry said he only had to go about fifteen feet deep and hit good water. He had even built a cover over it.

Yano thought of Elu every second of every day. His father would catch him daydreaming instead of working. Yano wanted to move into Sloppy's shanty, he had never looked for the treasure that Sloppy had written about being hidden in there somewhere. He had told his father and mother how he felt about Elu and in about two more weeks, he wanted to go back. He said he could check on his grandparents and stay with them too, while he was there.

Alan said, "I knew that was coming. I wish we could have met her when we were there. We did see her when she walked by that first day, she is a beautiful young lady, and I expect very nice too."

"Yes sir, she is very sweet, smart and a beautiful lady and had the same birthdate as me. We would never forget one another's birthday."

At only sixteen years old, Yano looked twenty with his broad shoulders, muscled arms, strong hands and stands about six feet tall. He had black hair and blue eyes and is the spitting image of his father, not only in appearance, but in his love of exploring, adventures and his willingness to help others in need.

As he sat on the bunk inside the shanty that Sloppy stayed in when he was with them, he was remembering the letters from Sloppy. He looked for the secret hiding place in the shanty, hoping there were more words from Sloppy there. He remembered Sloppy's words to look for something out of place. Yano had not looked for the secret hiding place in the shanty until now and couldn't see anything that looked out of place. He sought the spirit of Sloppy for help. Yano stood in front of a mirror that hung over the wash basin. His reflection was looking back at him. There was something wrong with the way the mirror hung, it was not centered with the wash basin. It would have been easy to center it up, but it was left off center, it looked out of place. Yano asked himself if the secret hiding place was looking him right in the face. He removed the mirror from the wall and found a piece of tin covering a hole cut out in the wall behind the mirror. It was about a six-inch circle with a collar for a stove pipe to go through. When he looked in the hole, he could not see anything except the exterior wall that had no hole for the stove pipe to exit through. He still thought this had to be the secret place. The hole was between the studs and a little off center of the wash basin. That could explain why the mirror was off center. Not seeing anything in the hole, he stuck his hand in it to feel around. His arm would only go so far, but he could reach the stud on his left and felt nothing. When feeling for the stud on the right, he felt a nail that had been nailed into the stud. The nail had a string tied to it and when he pulled on the string, he could feel some weight on the end of it. As he pulled the string up to the hole in the wall, there was a cloth bag tied to the end. Yano pulled the bag through the hole and untied the string. Yano just sat down, holding the bag. He was more interested in the papers than the coins because he knew they would have Sloppy's writing on them. Unfolding the papers, the first one read, *"Yano, by you reading this means you located the first hiding place, like I knew you would. At a young age, you were a good tracker and explorer that loved adventures. Don't let the treasures you find be your only treasure. Always let the hunt be just as important of a treasure as the one you may find. Share it with your family and always try to help those that need it. Keep learning how to survive without treasures. There is a thousand dollars in gold coins in this bag for you to use or share, however you choose. Keep some secrets in order to keep your family safe. Find yourself a soulmate that shares the same interest that you do. If you decide to be a mountain man, having a soulmate will keep the loneliness away."*

When Yano read the soulmate part, he could no longer read anymore, because he knew he had already found his soulmate. All he could think about now was Elu. He folded the papers up and placed them back in the bag with the gold coins. There was a lot more writing to read, but that would be for another time. He tied the string back to the bag and lowered it back down the hole, covering it with the piece of tin and hanging the mirror back just like it was.

Chapter 20

One week later, he was loaded up with his bedroll, a little food and two hundred dollars in gold coins in his pocket and riding to High Point. He would check on his grandparents, help with their chores while he was there, and try to spend as much time with Elu as he could. His mother had made him a beautiful necklace of friendship to give Elu. He was excited to see her reaction when he showed up and was hoping she was excited to see him as much as he was to see her.

When he arrived at his grandparents' home, they were very happy to see him, but they knew he really wanted to see Elu.

Yano asked them if they knew Elu and his grandmother said, "Yes, we know her and her parents. They are very good and honest people."

Yano said he hoped to meet her family on this trip.

Yano's grandmother Awinita said, "Elu's mother's name is Ahyoka and her father is Atsadi Walker. You should call them Mr. and Mrs. Walker, it shows respect."

He said, "Yes Ma'am".

"Her great grandmother is Omawi, she is known as the spirit reader."

He asked if they had any chores he could help with now before he went to the village to find Elu.

His grandmother said, "Yes, you could bring a little more stove wood and stack it on the porch, it's already cut, your grandfather's back is hurting him a little and he would appreciate you doing that for him."

Yano asked if it would be alright for him to stay with them for a few nights. That made them happy, and they said, "you can stay here Yano for as long as you like."

Yano finished up his chores and told his grandparents that he was going to the village to see Elu.

Grandmother Awinita said she would hold him out a plate of supper for when he returned, she knew it might be late.

He had removed the saddle from Smokie and would ride him bareback. When he got to the village, he rode up to the end where Granny Omawi was usually sitting on her porch. Omawi was not on the porch, but Elu's paint horse was tied out front. When he hopped off of Smokie and tied him to a post, Elu came running out of the cabin wearing the biggest smile and said, "Yano, you did come back, and I am so happy you did."

Yano asked if Omawi was alright.

Elu said, "Yes, we were just having some sassafras tea, come in to see her and have some tea with us."

Before they went in, Yano took the necklace his mother made out of his pocket and told Elu to close her eyes. He then placed the necklace over her head and told her to look. She said, "I love it and thank you for such a beautiful gift."

When they went inside, Granny Omawi saw the necklace and speaking in Cherokee said, "two spirits joined together," and smiled at them.

Yano thought Omawi approved of him, and he hoped her parents would to. Omawi is the elder great grandmother to Elu, so Yano asked for the right to court her. Omawi gave her permission and told Yano to tell her parents she had given approval. Yano asked Elu if he could meet her parents. "Yes, you can, my father is at work and won't be home until late, but we can go see my mother now."

Yano thanked Omawi for the tea and he and Elu rode to her house, so he could meet her mother. Elu's mother was sitting on their porch knitting a beautiful blanket when they arrived. She was educated and spoke perfect English, but she spoke in Cherokee to Yano saying, "You must be Yano, the one Elu talks so fondly of."

He spoke back in Cherokee and said, "Yes, Mrs. Walker, I am Yano, and I am very fond of Elu."

Mrs. Walker smiled at both of them and asked him in English, "Where are your parents and what is their name?"

Yano said, "My mother was raised in this village and her name is Odina Elu Adams."

Mrs. Walker said, "I know Odina, when we were young, we played together, we are friends, but have not seen each other in years."

"My father is Alan Atohi Adams, and we live fifty miles north of here in Shepherd Springs, West Virginia."

She said she knew Alan and his parents, James and Awinita Adams. "All are good people."

"Yes Ma'am, I think so too. That is a beautiful blanket you are knitting."

"Thank you, Yano, I sell them to the Trading Post in High Point. I am about finished with this one and I have three more to take to him."

Yano asked, how much for a blanket like that?"

She said, "I get two dollars for each one and he sells them for four dollars each."

Yano said he would really like to buy two of them and asked if she would sell him two of them.

She looked excited because he liked them and wanted to buy them and said, "Yes, two for four dollars and you pick them out."

Yano picked two blankets out and gave her a fifty-dollar gold piece.

Mrs. Walker looked at the fifty-dollar gold piece and said, "I don't have change for that Yano, here, I'll give these blankets to you."

"No Ma'am, I really like these blankets and don't want any change."

Elu told her mother to take it, "he wants to give you that extra money as a gift of friendship."

Mrs. Walker stood there in shock, "that much money would really help us buy food for the family."

Yano asked Elu if she wanted to ride over to her special place at the creek with many waterfalls.

She said, "Yes, she would like that very much."

Her mother told her to be back at supper time. "Yes Mother" she replied.

When they arrived at her special spot, they went to the large boulder on the creek and climbed up on top of it. Looking down at the pool of water, they could see several nice size trout. The water was crystal clear and cold. They were not even thinking of fishing today, just being together made them happy.

Elu asked Yano to tell her more about his friend Sloppy.

He said, "Sloppy's name was Willard Floyd, but everybody called him Sloppy, probably because the front of his shirt was always stained with tobacco juice. Sloppy was a true mountain man that lived on an eight-hundred-acre plat of land that he owned. The land is a two-day ride from our homeplace to his. He lived alone in the Appalachian Mountains for over forty years and would only come out every few months for supplies. Sloppy had many secrets that he kept to himself. I learned so much from Sloppy and will tell you more over the next fifty years."

Feeling the warmth of the sun as they lay on top of the boulder, they heard the call of a hawk. Yano could see a Red Tail Hawk circling high above in the sky and said, "that's Sloppy's spirit, it must have heard me talking about him."

Yano asked Elu if she would come to his grandparents tomorrow.

He said he would come to the village and ride with her.

She said, "Yes, it would be nice to see Mr. and Mrs. Adams, I have not seen them in a while."

He said, "good, I will help them with chores in the morning, then come to the village by nine to ride back there with you. I would like to go down to the Potomac River to fish and then do a little exploring."

Elu smiled and said, "that sounds good. I like to fish and explore." They were enjoying being together and learning more about each other. Yano looked downstream and could see a sandbar that had black sand in it. He had always been told that black sand was a good sign that gold was present in the area. He asked Elu if she or anybody else had ever searched for gold on the creek.

She answered, "No, I haven't and have never seen anyone in this area. People from the village go to the river to fish."

He said, "let's go downstream, I want to look at something." When they got to the sandbar, Yano scooped up a double handful of sand and small pebbles and spread it out on top of a large rock.

Elu spotted a few flakes of gold in his first scoop, and she was all excited. He tried to dig deeper because he knew that gold was heavier and would fall deeper. In the next scoop, they found more flakes. Yano explained to Elu the importance of secrecy of locations where gold was found. The wrong people could harm you if they heard there was gold here.

She said she understood. He scooped another scoop out and found more. He thought he could do much better with a shovel and a pan, but if seen with a shovel and pan, people would know that he was prospecting for gold. Yano said there was more gold there, but that was all the scooping with hands they would do today.

It was getting close to supper time, and he knew to respect her mother's order to be back by supper, so they walked back to their horses. Before mounting the horses, they kissed again, then he rode with her to her house before heading back to his grandparents.

The next day went great. They were able to catch enough fish for his grandparents and her family. Both enjoyed each other's company, fishing together and exploring together. They made arrangements to meet at her special place the next morning. He said he would borrow a gold pan and a shovel from his grandfather.

They both arrived at Elu's special place at the same time. They greeted each other with a kiss and with a shovel and pan in hand, they walked to where the black sand was to dig for gold. Yano was able to dig deeper with the shovel and he showed Elu how to swish the water around in the pan. With excitement in her voice she said, "Gold, there's lots of gold flakes in here"

Yano pulled a small tobacco pouch out of his pocket and told Elu to put all of the gold she found in it. They continued to dig for the next few hours and found more gold and a few small nuggets.

They had a great day, enjoying each other's company fishing, panning for gold and kissing each other. The kissing part was Yano's favorite part. He insisted that she keep all the gold they found to help her family. He told her not to tell anyone except her family of the location unless she wanted a lot of people showing up to prospect the area. "Call it a secret for safety."

Yano always hated leaving Elu and couldn't wait to return. He knew she would be waiting, but he also knew he would miss her and worry until he saw her again. He made the trip at least once a month even throughout the winter months, which were brutal with snow, ice and below freezing temperatures. Staying with his grandparents and helping them on each trip made him feel good and he always looked forward to seeing Omawi and listening to her wise guidance and spirit readings. Each trip, he met more of Elu's family and finally, after many trips, he had now met them all. They were good, hard-working people who knew what it was like to have little means to survive, but they did survive, because they understood and knew the Cherokee way they had learned from their ancestors. They all could see how happy he made Elu, but they also knew, the wise spirit reader, Omawi, who saw through the soul, had given her approval of Yano. That approval was most sacred to the Cherokee people.

Yano and Elu had talked many times about marriage and their future life together in the past few months. They each realized, though young in age, they were true soulmates, completely committed to each other. Since it had now been almost a year since they first met and they had the blessings of both families, they decided to get married on February 2, 1866, the day they both would celebrate their seventeenth birthday. Since they only had a short time left before the wedding, they had many things to do. They would be married in a traditional Cherokee wedding, which involved several ceremonies. There were items that would be needed to carry out each part of the ceremony. Omawi provided the list of the items needed and the order in which the tradition would follow. The families, the village and the elders all came together to help Yano and Elu make sure everything needed was on hand and ready for their wedding day.

The day had arrived, it was now February 2, 1866, and they were surrounded by both families, the elders and the village. The ceremony could now begin. As tradition, Omawi would perform the ceremony, and the elders would carry out her instructions.

Fire had always been considered sacred to the Cherokees, so Omawi began with the Sacred Fire Ceremony. She told the elders to make three fires from seven types of trees. The large fire in the center was for the Creator and the joining together of two souls. Next, one of the elders was told to lay wood for two small fires, one to the south and one to the north. One was for Yano, and one was for Elu. They all began to sing sacred songs and pray as Yano and Elu each lit their fires and slowly pushed them into the large fire. The fires then became one and they all sang praises to the Creator. After the Sacred Fire Ceremony, the Basket Ceremony followed, which represented both mothers' part in the wedding. Elu's mother brought Elu a basket with corn and bread. Yano's mother brought Yano a leg of cooked deer in a basket. The mothers then put a blue blanket over their child's shoulder and Yano and Elu were told to walk toward each other and look into each other's eyes. Elu took the corner of his blanket and folded it into her blanket and gave him her basket of corn and bread, which she showed her promise to keep their home and support her husband.

Yano handed Elu his basket of cooked deer, his promise to provide for her needs and protect her always from all harm.

Omawi said it was now time for the Cherokee Wedding Blanket Ceremony.

Yano's parents and Elu's parents were told to come forward with a large white blanket and put it over the shoulders of Yano and Elu. The blanket covered their weaknesses, any shame or sorrow and they were now joined in happiness and peace.

Omawi declared, "The blankets are joined." which was the official ending of the Cherokee Wedding Ceremony.

As the ceremony ended, Yano and Elu drew close together and looked up towards the mountains. Looking far into the distance, high above the mountains, perched on a huge rock, a beautiful Wolf appeared only to them.

They understood that their spirits were now officially joined together as one.

Omawi begans to speak the Cherokee Wedding Prayer which honored the three forces of nature; fire, wind and water as well as the blessings each brought to the marriage. All the family members, the elders and the village began a Stomp Dance to celebrate the marriage in true Cherokee custom. It had been a full day of celebration for Yano and Elu who were now officially man and wife. They both would always treasure the fact that their wedding was performed and blessed by Omawi in her 100th year of age.

Chapter 21

They lived their first year as a married couple, staying in the shanty that Sloppy stayed in when he was there at the Adam's homeplace. They had made many trips together to Sloppy's place in the Appalachians to explore together and pan for gold. Even though Sloppy left him his eight hundred acres of land and the cabin, he would always call it Sloppy's place. Every time they stayed at Sloppy's cabin in the Appalachian Mountains, A Red Tail Hawk would circle high in the sky over the cabin and Sloppy's grave. Yano knew that Sloppy's spirit was always with him.

Yano had taken up sitting on the porch and drinking coffee, just like his father and Sloppy. He understood now how relaxing it was to just sit there, listen to the sounds of the mountains, breathe the mountain air and think how blessed he was to have his soulmate by his side on this journey of life.

Elu's family had never prospected for gold, so before leaving to move to Shepherd Springs to live, she told her family of her special place. Elu wanted them to know there was enough gold there to help buy supplies and the food they needed. She told them it would be good for her brothers, Dustu and Dakota, to start prospecting, but warned them to keep the secret and not tell anyone. She worried it would become crowded with prospectors and it could put her family in harm.

Yano always helped his father with tending the cattle along with taking them to market to sell. There were many other chores that had to be done on the land, also, but he never complained, he loved the land and appreciated all that he had. When he cameshome from a hard day's work, he was always greeted with the most beautiful smile from his beautiful wife.

Every few months, they would ride down to High Point to check on his grandparents and Elu's family. Once the first trip back, Dustu and Dakota couldn't wait to tell Elu about their prospecting and the gold they found right where she told them to look. This is great news to her because she knows that her family can find enough gold to carry them through the hard times.

Sitting on the porch this evening, Yano thought back to his childhood days. He remembered all the things his father and mother had taught him. Even at a young age, he had the desire to explore and go on adventures. He thought back to when his father gave him his first test of manhood and all the tests that came after that. He learned how to treat people by listening and watching his parents and Sloppy. He was always taught to help people in need and stay away from the bad ones. Sloppy left him several letters and notes on how to live his life. He treasured them all, especially the part where Sloppy said, "find your soulmate to do life with". He knew he had found her.

Elu and he would spend a lot of their time staying at the cabin at the lake. While he was on the other end of the land working, she would stay at the cabin and explore. This was a very special place for both of them because the Spirit of the Wolf was always present here. They had enlarged the corral a little, providing a little more room for their horses and would live in the cabin for a few months at a time or longer if they wished.

One afternoon, when Yano returned to the cabin, Elu was not at the cabin to greet him like she usually was. He panicked at the thought of something happening to her while he was gone and then he thought about the beautiful lake behind the cabin. Elu loved the water and fell in love with this lake the first time she saw it and loved to swim in it. He started walking toward the lake and approached the large rock that they usually sat on to fish, swim or just think. He was amazed at what he is witnessing. Elu was completely nude sitting there, staring out at the water and a large Wolf was sitting next to her. She had her right arm draped over the Wolf's neck and shoulder area. Both seemed to be meditating. The first and only time that he was able to touch the Wolf was several years ago and on the other side of the lake while he was sitting on top of a large rock. As he got closer, he could see her clothes lying on the rock at her left side. She had been swimming as she had done many times before and was letting the warmth of the sun dry her. He quietly climbed up on top of the rock and sat beside this large Wolf. It never attempted to move or run. Now they had this large Wolf in between them as he draped his left arm over the Wolf's shoulder. He looked at his beautiful wife, they both smiled, and he could feel the fur of the Wolf against his arm and smell its smell. The Wolf was just staring out across the lake like he was protecting her by standing guard.

"He leaned across the top of the Wolf and gave his wife a long kiss." When their lips parted, the Wolf was gone. They never felt him move or heard a sound. He just vanished like before. No tracks were found, and he didn't think they ever would be, because the Spirt of the Wolf leaves no sign.

The End

www.ingramcontent.com/pod-product-compliance
Lightning Source LLC
Chambersburg PA
CBHW061536120726
48001CB00004B/1582